Loaded Questions

BY THE SAME AUTHOR

Death Wishes
Sea-Change
Wrong Man in the Mirror
Voices in an Empty Room
Photographs Have Been Sent to Your Wife
A Mafia Kiss
W.I.L. One to Curtis

PHILIP LORAINE

Loaded Questions

St. Martin's Press
New York

LOADED QUESTIONS. Copyright © 1985 by Philip Loraine.
All rights reserved. Printed in the United States of America. No part of this book may be used or reproduced in any manner whatsoever without written permission except in the case of brief quotations embodied in critical articles or reviews. For information, address St. Martin's Press, 175 Fifth Avenue, New York, N.Y. 10010.

Library of Congress Cataloging in Publication Data

Loraine, Philip, pseud.
  Loaded questions.

  I. Title.
PR6062.067L6   1986   823'.914   85-25160
ISBN 0-312-49340-1

First published in Great Britain by William Collins Sons & Co. Ltd.
First U.S. Edition
10 9 8 7 6 5 4 3 2 1

Part One

LONDON

'They think they have power, but we're the ones who make them and break them.'

1

Savage Mediterranean sun behind a thin gauze of cloud. The whole city sodden with heat, a dead heat, even at ten o'clock in the morning. In front of the Hotel Imperia drooping tourists, fanning themselves with the day's itinerary, were being swallowed one after the other by their panting coach; it trembled with the effort, for its motor was running, and a shimmering haze of heat surrounded it. Dead heat, dead morning, morning of death.

The three cars and the six motorcycle policemen drew up at the side entrance at ten minutes past ten. Late. Security men burst from the cars like hefty children released from school, almost hiding the frail and elderly man who climbed out more slowly, glanced up at the glaring sky and grimaced to himself. He didn't look important; his suit, a little too large in any case, was already rumpled so early in the day, and his face was rumpled too, by many years of persecution and struggle against odds. He looked as if he should be ambling across a campus towards some distant lecture-hall, or tending his tomatoes at home, and no doubt would have preferred to be doing either.

The security phalanx moved at his speed up the steps, under the canopy, through the double doors, into the aseptic modernity of the vast lobby where even the largest indoor plant seemed lost, writhing towards a ceiling it would never reach.

The young man turned from watching the slow procession, his face taut with anger. He was hidden from them by a screen of carefully tended vegetation: the ugly swords of Sanseveria, pointless abundance of Ficus Elastica, slashed leaves of Monstera, rampaging ivy everywhere. He had loathed and feared indoor plants ever since that day. A honey-bee, lost in the man-made jungle, crawled bemusedly across a Monstera leaf, avoiding the chasms. The young man was watching it, thinking that they had a lot in common, himself and the bee, when the Assistant Manager came up behind him and spoke his name.

It was the old worry: would the conference be over by Thursday week when the ballroom must be prepared for this prestigious party to be given by some Principessa whose family had been honoured clients, etcetera, etcetera? The young man was still protesting that the matter had nothing to do with him—better call Washington and ask the President of the United States—when the first shot cracked the muffled heat somewhere behind him, followed by another.

Presumably he turned on the instant, but it seemed as if all eternity lumbered by before he plunged through the palisade of greenery, leaving havoc behind him, and ran across the useless wastes of the lobby. Nobody else was moving, or even in sight, yet a few minutes earlier there had seemed to be people everywhere. Presumably they were now lying flat on the floor.

Enormous plate-glass doors led into a wide passage, lit from one side by recessed windows. Between bars of cloud-filtered sunlight he saw scuttling shadows and, closer to him, the old man turning slowly, arms outspread, a surprised expression on his face.

The doors were locked, as they should have been, but nothing else was as it should have been. Perhaps he ought to have taken exact note of what was happening in the passage, but this he could not do while carefully aiming at the lock with a .38. He fired (third shot—there was to be a lot of counting of shots, a lot of pointless analysis). The left-hand door disintegrated in an avalanche of glass; its pair swung open automatically, sedately, but by that time he was flinging himself forward. At the same moment he heard the crack of another shot (the fourth). As he caught the old man, blood came choking from his mouth; he felt it on his face and between their clenched bodies, welding them together.

He saw, beyond the old man's bloodied face, a moving figure; managed to raise the .38 and fire it (fifth shot); the figure veered off sideways, either wounded or taking evasive action. The sixth and last shot hit the young man's right arm; his gun sailed away and went slithering along the polished marble floor into illimitable distance. He staggered backwards, still refusing to relinquish the heavy weight of his obligation. Then something struck him viciously on top of the head and he began to fall. They went down, he and the old man, in a welter of arms and legs and blood and, adding insult to fatal injury, more revolting indoor plants, snapping and squelching and slapping his face and becoming inextricably entangled with his neck and with the old man's dangling arms . . .

. . . and the plants had developed faces, or parts of faces, a staring eye here, a gaping mouth there. They had also developed a savage life of their own; swords of Sanseveria were jabbing at him, and the slobbering lips of rubber plants pressed themselves against his mouth, stifling him with wet lascivious kisses. He was naked. Tendrils of ivy wrapped themselves around his body and pulled at his penis. Ivy was sprouting from his belly, he could feel the burgeoning shoots pressing at the backs of his eyeballs, he was being devoured by vegetation, he was screaming . . .

Holly Lathan was wide awake at the very instant that her husband cried out. Sometimes she wondered if a sixth sense didn't warn her a split second before he cried out. She switched on the bedside light, hoping that its glare would wake him, but apparently this terror only attacked in the deepest of sleep or, since we are told that the deepest of sleep is dreamless, somewhere very near the edge of it. He was rolling his head this way and that, and his cheeks were wet with tears. As so often before.

She put an arm under the pillow and drew him towards

her; Dr Vercours, whom she trusted, had warned her never to wake him abruptly. Steve Lathan seemed unwilling to wake at all, almost as if he preferred his nightmare to everyday life. It astonished her how young he looked in sleep, even when so obviously distraught: fair hair tousled, tear-stained face as smooth as a boy's. At first he struggled to escape from her, and he was strong; but so was she, and gradually her strength impressed itself upon him; he wasn't alone in his fear; somebody was close to him, somebody whom he could trust, love . . .

He gave a deep sigh and opened his eyes. Blue, puzzled eyes fixed on hers, which were brown and perspicacious. 'Old knowing-eyes,' he sometimes said. 'Holly's only twenty-four but her eyes are as old as Time.'

'Oh God! Was I hollering?'

'You were hollering.' She had never got used to any of his Americanisms and often echoed them in a kind of amused yet childish wonder. 'Hollering fit to bust.'

How strange that now, when terror had given way to the old self-mocking smile, he should look so much older: a tough, even slightly battered, man of thirty-six. 'Hollering and crying.' She reached for a tissue and dried his cheeks. She loved him very much for not pretending about the tears, wiping them ashamedly on the sheet or protesting that they'd never existed as an Englishman would probably have done.

'What is it, Steve? Why can't you tell me?'

'Honey, I don't *know* what it is.'

She knew this wasn't true; the straightforwardness which she loved was shot through with all manner of evasions which frightened her; a part of him was forever shut away behind a locked door. He had been perfectly honest about this, had explained it to her patiently when they first fell in love. She was thus confronted by a contradiction in terms: straightforward evasion. When he said, 'I don't know what it is,' he meant, 'It belongs to the time I don't talk about.'

All right, she had accepted that, no option, but she had never accepted the fact that the nightmare recurred and recurred. 'I hesitate,' Dr Vercours had said, 'to talk about . . . psychiatry.'

So then she had been forced to tell him: it was nothing to do with the subconscious, on the contrary it was something to do with a memory which, most consciously, he would not admit to having. At which Dr Vercours had shaken his head and spread his hands in a very French gesture of resignation. The spread hands said, 'In that case the matter is out of my hands.'

Steve Lathan now smiled and pulled her dark head down to his fair one on the pillow. 'Don't frown like that, the wind might change.' She knew that he would make love to her and was glad of it; not because she felt particularly sexy, shocked awake by an agonized cry at five in the morning, but because she knew that love-making was for him a reaffirmation of life after whatever death he had lived through in his sleep.

When they had made love they made coffee. It was past 6.0 a.m. Paris was on the move all about them; workmen were swigging a 'fine' in the café on the corner; the Métro (Nation-Concorde) shot out of its tunnel on to what Steve called 'the elevated' above the Boulevard Garibaldi; they only heard it for a few seconds as it passed the far end of their street, Rue Mannin; Holly had grown to love the sound, as indeed she had grown to love living in Paris.

'Paris!' her British friends cried. 'But it's so expensive, it's dirty, the Parisians hate everybody.'

No use protesting that it was nowhere near as expensive as London, and much better value; that it was twice as clean; that Parisians, who never suffered fools gladly, preferred people who spoke a little of their own language, however badly.

'Do you know,' her friends would say to each other later,

'Olivia's a *francophile*!' Cannibalism or witchcraft would have seemed to them less reprehensible.

As for the 'Olivia', it was her husband who had insisted on discarding it: 'Okay, I'm a hick American, but I can't spend the rest of my life calling you Olivia, I'd have to touch my forelock every time.'

Ollie? They were neither of them that addicted to Laurel and Hardy. Holly? Yes, he liked that. Nice and prickly to go with her nature!

There was a small table in front of their kitchen window; they always drank their coffee sitting on either side of it, looking directly down the street towards the 'elevated'. They loved this street.

'The Comtesse de la Grande-Poitrine is early. Do you know, Steve, she *taps* all the loaves before buying one.' The lady in question bore the bosom in question with proud vigour; Holly, coming up behind her in the market, had nearly been knocked flying when the Comtesse turned abruptly.

'Monsieur Souris with his extra-large briefcase. Holly, he's got to be a pusher.'

She shook her head. 'Income Tax. Hence the furtive look.'

'Maybe he's got the whole department hooked—that's why their letters never make sense.'

The hands that were not holding the giant coffee-cups lay on the table, clasped. Hers seemed frail and helpless inside his, but this was misleading; she was by no means either frail or helpless. Did he really know, she asked herself yet again, how much she valued his love and cherished it: the more so because he had given up a whole life, a whole career, in order to marry her? What if he did have secrets on the far side of their falling in love? So had she, oh God, so had she! Then why did he writhe and weep in the grip of terrible nightmares while she slept so peacefully, the sleep of the unjust? This often asked and unanswerable question made her squeeze his hand, so hard that he glanced at her in surprise.

She said, 'I love you. I didn't know people kept saying that after centuries of being married.'

'Come back to bed, I'll give you centuries!'

'No. You'll run smack into the rush-hour, it's time you were dressed.'

'It's time I took *you* away from France, you're getting a lot too practical.'

He had to drive out to Sannois, a northern suburb. His wife, since as yet they had no children, worked as secretary to a showy and no doubt shady film financier with a glamourous office on the Champs-Elysées: Golden Promotions et Cie. He held an American passport but was otherwise, in every conceivable respect, Hungarian.

Looking out of the window, Holly said, 'You're usually in the shower by the time Pépé le Moko comes out of the café.'

He stretched and yawned and moved away towards the bathroom. Watching him, strong legs still faintly tanned from last year's sun, fair hair standing on end where he'd slept on it, she thought that possibly it was the secrets which kept them happy, supplying a kind of tension, an eternal strangeness. In marriage, perhaps, it was not a little knowledge which was a dangerous thing, but too much knowledge, too great a certainty.

2

Tom Wood was leaning on the counter at El Vino, a bar in Fleet Street, in London. He had a hangover, the kind that never goes away until it has been outpaced by more alcohol, and he was resenting the fact that the place was full of journalists, a futile resentment, that being its prime purpose in life; and anyway he was a journalist himself.

He wished he had given today a miss and stayed in bed. No, he didn't wish that because his bed, when vacated, had been occupied by somebody called Henrietta, rendering it no place for peaceful relaxation. She had shown no inclination to get up when he did, but in half darkness with the hangover thudding at his skull, he had gained a swift impression of tumbled auburn hair and a slim young body (a bit too young when he considered it later), definitely attractive, thank God alcohol didn't rob him of taste in that direction. However, it was high time he learned to come back from parties alone; the last thing he needed after an over-convivial evening was to wake up and find that he wasn't in sole possession. And oh God, he must get out of this damned pub, full of pretentious hacks bolstering their egos in loud and querulous voices.

He straightened up from his corner. Since he was a very large young man, and known to be of unreliable temper when inebriated, nearby querulous hacks drew back slightly as he pushed towards the door. One or two of them hailed him by name but he ignored them. Somebody said, 'Pissed again! Isn't it getting a bit boring?' Wood ignored that also.

He knew he was being unreasonable; he had arranged to meet his friend and partner, David Cameron, in this bar at one o'clock, and it was still only ten to; on the other hand Cameron wouldn't really want to have lunch with him in his present state, and there were plenty of old gossips to report on the state he was in, so he was really doing both a favour by disappearing.

A gust of cold wind met him in the street; March was declining to give way to April. Wood took deep breaths of it and immediately felt better. He headed for Covent Garden, for a small and unfashionable pub left over from the days when the Garden had been a market, not a tourist-trap; it would be full of ordinary people, none of them pretending to be anything else.

Had be possessed full control of his faculties, as the good investigative journalist he was, he would have been aware of the fact that a man had been waiting for him outside El Vino and was now following him; but then, if he had been in full control of his faculties the man would have known it and would have taken good care to conceal himself, he was a professional: thin, unremarkable, wearing an unremarkable dark grey suit; his hair was cut short and grew in a slight widow's peak which accentuated the pallor of his bony face.

Tom Wood went into The Duck. The unremarkable man presently followed. Wood ordered a large Scotch and chatted up the barmaid who was pretty; the unremarkable man ordered a Perrier and ran Tom Wood through his mind like tape through a recorder:

> WOOD, Thomas Carver Cavendish. Son of General (retired) Sir Richard and Lady Wood of Astley Manor, Wiltshire. Age 26. Height 6ft 3ins. Weight 14 stone. Hair. light brown, straight. Eyes, greenish. Distinguishing mark, six-inch scar on back of left shoulder-blade—riding accident. Religion, none (i.e. C of E). Hobbies: girls, drinking, theatre, classical music and trad-jazz. Sports: tennis and sailing. Politics, Conservative. Car, seven-year-old blue Deux Chevaux.
>
> Educated at Eton and Trinity College, Cambridge. Left university after one year: rebellious youth, anti-Establishment (but still Conservative) etc., etc. Went to London to become a journalist. Achieved this ambition by capitalizing on some of his father's old friendships and by playing his cards intelligently. Worked as tea-boy, errand-boy, general dogsbody, for three years, waiting for a break.
>
> Break came in the shape of CAMERON, David Brian (see separate file), inferior socially, superior academically, equally ambitious, and in the shape of chance remark

which led the two reporters to the Vatican Bank Scandal. Exclusive. A sensation.

Not all assignments equally successful, but partners established as leading investigative reporting team in Britain, perhaps Europe.

The Duck, not to mention the pretty barmaid, induced in Tom Wood a more equable frame of mind; or it might have been the Scotch, he was catching up with himself. He left the pub and wandered along Bow Street, turned into Long Acre and headed for the Garrick Club. Enough of the pushy world, he suddenly desired a little not too exclusive exclusivity. It was now one-forty; most of the members would be in the Dining Room extending their, for the most part already well-extended, waistlines.

The pale man with the slight widow's peak watched him disappear from sight. Members only. He turned and walked away.

Wood washed himself thoroughly, face included, combed his hair, exchanged a few racing tips. Ten minutes later he ascended to the bar, looking, feeling, almost being, a new man. As he had supposed, the room was nearly empty; at one end of the counter three members were congratulating themselves on some business deal; at the other, lost in thought, leaned a smart and uncommunicative-looking man. Wood ordered the bartender's hangover special and, in doing so, caught his neighbour's eye. The man said, 'Like that, eh?'

'I'm afraid so.'

The eyes which appraised him were black and bright. The suit was faultless, the tie correctly subdued, the shirt-cuffs just so, the grey hair expertly barbered. Wood guessed that he was a very successful publisher or a somewhat swinging banker; no other kind of banker would have been found dead inside the Garrick. He introduced himself. 'Wood, Tom Wood.'

'The reporter? *Follow-Up?*'

No use pretending it didn't give one a warm and cosy glow. 'Yes.'

'You've done some good things.' Incisive. Implying others less good. 'My name's John Merrion.' A very slight smile indicated that he was aware of the younger man's curiosity which the younger man thought he was concealing. 'East-West Airspace, if you're interested. Rather boring compared with your job.'

Well, if 'boring' meant an obviously high executive salary within one of the major international companies, limitless free air travel, accommodation in any of East-West's one hundred and seventeen luxury hotels all over the world—yes, it might be called boring, everything was a matter of degree.

For a long time the *Follow-Up* team had been considering a really swingeing attack on price-rigging and cheap-competitor-bashing inside the world's airlines, including a karate-chop at IATA. John Merrion of East-West Airspace, Inc. and Ltd., looked like being an interesting lead: if treated with extreme caution, for he would certainly guess what was going on.

They had a drink together, talking of foreign cities and restaurants, and the economics of air travel. They lunched together, talking of the balance between politics and the big multi-nationals, of theatre in Japan, the beauties of Siena, and the economics of air travel. They touched on strikes, terrorists and hijackers and their effect on the economics of air travel. At which point Mr Merrion, perhaps weary of parrying all this undercover interrogation, said, 'Have you ever done terrorism?'

'Difficult thing to research.'

'No more difficult than the airlines, I assure you.'

Tom Wood laughed. Not much else he could do.

'I met a terrorist once,' said Merrion reflectively. 'Sat next to him on one of our own planes, as a matter of fact.'

'Really? How did it start? Did he turn to you and say, "Hi! What's your job? I'm a terrorist"?'

'Actually I took him for something diplomatic, he seemed to know everything that was going on. A very smooth fellow.'

'Who was he, would I have heard of him?'

'Sayed Duval.'

'God, yes. Libyan. Didn't he ... What was it—quite a few years ago?'

'He didn't tell me who he was, of course. Then, a couple of months later, after that nasty business in Frankfurt, I saw his picture in the paper. Recognized him at once.'

'Yes, Frankfurt. But something else too.'

'When I look back on it I realize he's been involved in most of their dirty work.'

'Got it!' said Wood. 'That Israeli, Isaac Erter, the peace man. Assassinated. In Rome, wasn't it?'

'I believe he mentioned that. Flatly denied the Libyans were involved.'

'Lying. Why not?'

'No, I don't think so. He seemed ... kind of upset. *Amour propre*, almost.'

'I wonder if there's a story.'

'That's why I mentioned it—as well as to get you off the poor old airlines.'

'No, I don't mean terrorism—Isaac Erter. I don't believe it was ever properly explained.'

'To tell you the truth I don't know much about it. I think I was living in Hong Kong at the time.'

They talked about Hong Kong and its precarious future; and all the time Tom Wood was aware of that little mouse of an idea which had popped out of a hole in his memory and was now scuttling about under the floorboards of his mind. Sayed Duval—Isaac Erter.

When they parted he hurried excitedly to the telephone and called his office. Daisy, shared secretary, told him that Mr Cameron had not been best pleased to be stood up at

El Vino, had judged from available evidence that no work would be done that afternoon, and had gone home.

Mr John Merrion, when they parted, crossed Garrick Street, walked a little way up Long Acre and got into a Mercedes parked on a meter. Sitting patiently behind the wheel was the pale and unremarkable man who had followed Wood from El Vino.

3

In their neat little house, modern Georgian, in Holland Park ('rather bourgeois for dedicated Socialists, isn't it?' Wood has asked, mocking) David and Shirley Cameron were bathing their children when the telephone rang. Cameron uttered a few curt 'yes's' and 'no's' into the receiver, replaced it, and said, 'Tom. Excited. He's coming round, I hope you don't mind.'

'I'd hardly tell you if I did. And of course I don't.'

Lucy, aged four, said, 'I want Uncle Tom to put me to bed.'

'You and all the other girls,' her mother replied tartly, smacking a pink behind. 'And brush your teeth properly.'

'Why? You said they were all going to fall out.'

Patrick, aged three, and showing every sign of a similar precocity, evidently considered this rejoinder the funniest thing he'd ever heard. Shirley sighed. 'Because I say so.' And to her husband, 'What's he excited about?'

'God knows.'

'I thought you said he was drunk.'

'A couple of old drunks in El Vino told me he was drunk.'

'Ugh! I can't think why you go there.'

'No need to be feminist, they admitted women ages ago.'

'On élitist terms. And I *am* feminist.'

David Cameron had been born in a dull cathedral town

where his father owned a small electrical shop. Having spent most of his own youth repairing vacuum-cleaners which had been used to pick up coins or pieces of Leggo, and kettles which had been allowed to boil themselves dry, Mr Cameron was determined to give his son the advantages he'd never had himself. He therefore sent him to the old grammar school which somehow, up until then, had managed to resist the more destructive plans of inept educationalists.

Unlike many boys from humble backgrounds whose fathers are determined to give them the advantages they'd never had themselves, young David worked very hard indeed, weathering the rude names and harsh tribal punishments meted out to hardworking boys by their dimmer peers; he had won himself a grant to a minor university where he read History and obtained a first-class degree. Somewhere along the way he also found time to meet and marry Shirley (Economics).

His father had been appalled—as appalled as, for instance, Sir Richard Wood in different circumstances—to find that his son wanted above all else to be a journalist. But what David wanted David, self-evidently, got; and his ambition, after biding its time throughout the usual teaching jobs and stints on provincial newspapers, finally hoisted him into Fleet Street and planted a flag on the peak.

At this point things came to a standstill. What was now required was some kind of catalyst. In another building not half a mile away Tom Wood was also kicking his heels, also growing weary of readers' letters and minor court cases, also waiting for a catalyst. The extraordinary thing was that Fortune, a wayward lady at the best of times, not only contrived a meeting between the two young men but ensured that they should recognize in each other the required virtue.

Less than a week later Wood bumped into a certain green young banker, Eton and Trinity, and he inadvertently made a remark which was to lead the two reporters, via weeks of gruelling research on minimum expenses, to the discovery of a number of surprising bank accounts held by inmates of the Vatican: and to equally surprising success. *Follow-Up* had been born.

But although it was a chance remark which had originated their celebrity, some of Wood's subsequent speculations had proved less inspired; which was why David Cameron wore a sceptical expression as he listened to his partner's description of lunch at the Garrick Club with somebody called John Merrion and of the conversation which had led his thoughts, via Sayed Duval, the terrorist, to the death of Isaac Erter. Clearly he did not find Wood's excitement contagious.

Cameron wore horn-rimmed glasses, which suited him. With his dark curly hair, his bony good looks and his sagging tweed suits he could have passed for an earnest young professor at the kind of university which had produced him. He boasted the right kind of Socialism for the part and even, on occasion, smoked a terrible pipe. When Wood's recitation was over he said, 'I don't get it.'

'Sayed Duval told this man that he had nothing to do with the assassination of Isaac Erter.'

'So? What's the story?'

'The story is, if the Libyans didn't kill him who did?'

'PLO, Red Brigade, KGB, practically any Arab who . . .'

'He was pro-Arab.'

'Rubbish! He was an Israeli.'

'He was the nearest thing to pro-Arab of any Israeli who ever lived.'

Cameron spread both hands. 'I'm sorry, Tom, the idea doesn't turn me on. It's too diffuse, it happened five years ago, it . . . it simply isn't important enough.'

Shirley, flushed from the exertion of getting Lucy and Patrick into bed and ensuring that they stayed there, joined them saying, 'What isn't important enough?'

'The death of Isaac Erter. For us, for a story.'

'*Not important enough!*' Shirley was a plump, pretty, soft-looking girl, not the kind given to flaring up at the drop of a hat or, as in this case, a name. 'David Cameron, who the bloody hell do you think you *are*?'

'Shirley, this is a technical . . .'

'Technical balls! Erter was the only man, *the only man*, who could have saved Israel . . .'

Tom Wood said, 'Let him have it, Shirley!'

'Who else ever had the guts to say that Israel's got one chance of survival, coming to terms with the Arabs instead of fighting them? Endless, stupid, mindless killing.'

'Atta–Shirl!'

'He wanted Israel to be a *country*, not a fortress. He was worth Meier and Ben-Gurion and all the rest of them rolled into one. Not important enough!'

There was a pause.

'Well,' said Wood, 'if that's any guide to the reaction of the Upwardly Mobile Young Married I'd say we had a winner.'

'What's the story?'

'David, people kill people for a *reason*. If the Arabs killed him it's a story, because he was the only Israeli friend they ever had.'

'Personally,' said Shirley, 'I think the Israelis did it themselves—organized by some prime pot-head like Dayan or Begin or Ariel Sharon. God, that country's crawling with fascists.'

'Okay, say the Israelis killed him, it's an even better story.'

More thoughtfully, Cameron said, 'Wasn't there some kind of Official Inquiry?'

'My God, yes!' His wife was off again. 'And *they* should have been shot, every single one of them!'

'Cover-up?'

'From here to Timbuctoo. Don't you remember? What were *you* doing?'

'Courting you, probably. Full-time job.'

'Could've fooled me.'

'Okay, Tom.' Cameron pushed the horn-rimmed glasses up his nose, always a sign of emotion; he liked cover-ups.
'Maybe we ought to go down to the library and check it out.'
'That's my boy!'
'But you're a rotten host,' said Shirley, 'it's ten past drinks-time.'
Cameron kissed her cheek. 'I thought you were giving it up in favour of a waistline.'
'I've been slugging it out with the Dead End Kids, I need gin.'

Shirley Cameron was an excellent cook, which accounted for her unfashionable figure. It was midnight before Wood got back to his flat on the top floor of a converted warehouse overlooking the Pool of London. He paused for a moment outside the door, listening nervously, for there had been occasions when the girl of the night before had elected to stay for more of the same. The idea of young Henrietta, satisfactory though she had been in many respects, waiting up for his return with an expectant expression made him feel old and faint-hearted; it had been a long day with which to follow a roistering night.

Hearing no sound he entered with confidence, switching on lights. A note was propped up on the large deal table which served as a desk:

Dear Tom—I thought the place looked a bit of a mess so I tidyed it up don't you have a claening lady or maybe you like it that way if so I'm soory I also maid you a nice new bed!!! ask me again sometime it was fun
                                                                Henrietta

Expensive education, so no knowledge whatever of spelling or punctuation, and undoubtedly a touch of fashionable dyslexia to go with it, but a nice girl.

The flat consisted of one huge room, with bathroom and kitchen and an ever-changing view of the river. Though Wood preferred its usual muddle—much easier to find things—he had to admit that it made a pleasant change to see it looking spick and span. He did indeed have a cleaning lady, very expensive and bone-idle; perhaps he could employ Henrietta instead, perhaps she'd like to move in for a while.

No, freedom was not to be bartered for a little cleanliness; nor indeed for anything else. He was thinking about Isaac Erter who had bartered it only for death.

4

The library was housed in the basement: air-conditioned peace after the clamour and tribulation of the floors above where next Sunday's edition was suffering its weekly labour-pains. Cameron and Wood sat side by side at two viewing machines amid miles of neatly indexed microfilm, winding, rewinding, making notes, starting, stopping, swearing, rewinding, until their brains reeled with print, their wits were addled, and their eyes crossed.

It seemed that Isaac Erter, man of peace, had arisen phoenix-like out of the flames of war: Israel versus Egypt, versus the Palestinians, Lebanon, Syria, versus anything Arab that raised its head. Not only wars and minor 'conflicts', but bombs and terrorists and hijackers, women gunned down, children blown to pieces. Shirley Cameron had been right: 'endless, stupid, mindless killing'.

It was hardly surprising that when Erter stood up in the Knesset and cried out, 'I want to live in a *country*, not in a blockhouse waiting for the next attack,' he was voicing the fervent desire of thousands of his fellow countrymen. When the hawks attacked him with tearing beaks and claws, as they naturally did, that murmuration of doves swelled louder and louder until, by a miracle, it overrode the harsh screeching of the birds of prey. Suddenly it seemed that a majority wanted peace, a majority wanted to live in a country, not in a blockhouse.

So Isaac Erter found himself propelled towards a kind of power he had never desired and was perhaps too old to carry. He celebrated his sixty-eighth birthday a week before his death. He accepted leadership of the Peace Party not because he wanted to rule—that was the last thing he wanted to do—but because he saw it as his moral duty; a man could hardly strive for something all his life and then turn his back on it when it had a chance of achieving success.

He initiated a 'dialogue', smart word at that 'moment of time', with the ancestral enemy: amid screams of hatred and derision from his antagonists, including many Jewish people in the United States.

The US Government found itself in an awkward position. For many years it had been spending millions of dollars daily in an effort to keep Israel afloat; it had also spent quite a few young American lives. But its Israeli allies were men of war, not men of peace, hawks, not doves. The President could hardly abandon those allies now, but neither could he afford to turn his back on what had come to be known as 'The Erter Initiative'. After all, everybody in the world wanted peace. Well, didn't they?

It was with mixed personal feelings, no doubt, and to a very mixed reception, that he decided to back Isaac Erter; or perhaps his flock of advisers could come up with no face-saving reason for *not* backing Isaac Erter.

An Israeli-Arab conference was convened, the first of this magnitude, certainly the first with a remote chance of success. The United Nations was woken gently from its sleep and coaxed into presiding, the chosen city was Rome, the chosen place the new Hotel Imperia (minimum security risk), and from the start Providence seemed to smile on the proceedings. It was not long before the gloomiest of all political correspondents was writing, 'No doubt about it, there is now a possibility of peaceful solution which would have seemed absurd six months ago.' This state of affairs was brought about by the simplest, most obvious, and most unpopular means: Isaac Erter agreed, without reservation, that territory must immediately be supplied or vacated upon which the Palestinians might found a homeland just as the Jews had founded a homeland not many years before.

Suddenly it seemed possible, despite howls of rage from extremists of every persuasion, that the whole monstrous problem could be settled, without any more loss of life, around a table in the converted ballroom of the Hotel Imperia in Rome. And if this was so, was it not also possible that the rest of the agonized and disintegrating world, which could be seen committing suicide any night on any television news, might at last regain its senses and turn towards the light of reason? Hope raised a cautious head that June, and was not for once shot dead on sight; and Isaac Erter became the human embodiment of this hope.

Then the bubble burst. Somebody destroyed the great possibility ('put the clock back fifty years', 'introduced a note of reality', 'wrecked the Middle East's only chance', 'restored Israel's pride'—each to his taste) by killing Erter on his way to the conference table.

In the library, at this point, there was a great deal of winding and rewinding punctuated by obscenities. David Cameron said, 'I can't even make out *how* it happened, can you?'

'Fuzzy. Very. "Our correspondent reports that the cars carrying Mr Erter and his security guards were held up by rush-hour traffic . . ."'

'With six motorcycle cops in attendance?'

'Oh well—Rome. ". . . rush-hour traffic, and were ten minutes late on arrival at the Hotel Imperia. What occurred next is unclear, but it seems possible that minutes before the shooting began Mr Erter *became separated from his escort*." Sounds like *Alice in Wonderland*!'

'Certainly doesn't sound like Israeli security.'
They continued their search. After a time Cameron said, 'Ah, a name, Tom! An actual name. 'Mr Steven Lathan, an American, who was off-duty at the time . . ."'

'Off-duty from what?'

'Doesn't say. "'. . . made an attempt to save the life of the Israeli leader and was himself shot. An Embassy spokesman said that Mr Lathan was in Intensive Care and unable to answer questions. It seems certain, however, that he is an important witness."'

Further winding and rewinding, but no making of notes or reading of paragraphs. The machines came to a standstill; the two young men looked at each other in astonishment. Cameron said, 'I don't believe it. There's absolutely no real information, just yards of non-news.'

'Quite a lot of recrimination going on between the different security outfits—Israelis blaming the Yanks and vice-versa, both of them blaming the Italians, everybody blaming the Arabs.'

'To paraphrase an immortal hooker, "They would, wouldn't they?" Where does your friend Sayed Duval come in, leading assorted Libyans?'

'Where indeed? The good old Department Of Afterthoughts, by the look of it.'

More searching. Cameron found it first. 'You're dead right. Erter was killed on the . . . what?'

'14th June.'

'And on the *24th* June . . . How's this? "A CIA official has confirmed that the Agency warned the Italian Government as early as 7th May that Sayed Duval, the Libyan terrorist leader, had been sighted in both Milan and Rome."'

Wood added to this: '27th June, minor headline: "Libyans Claim Responsibility for Death of Isaac Erter."'

Cameron laughed. 'Oh God, we're well away now. Talk about afterthoughts! 29th June: "At a special Press conference held at the headquarters of the Carabinieri, Signor Tullio said that Communist involvement in the death of Isaac Erter could not be ruled out. Experts were of the opinion that there were unmistakable similarities between this assassination and the attempt, some years ago, on the life of Pope John Paul II." I suppose it's possible —we'd better look into it.'

While he was making a note Wood said, 'Sweet Jesus! How's this for the pay-off? 4th July: "In answer to questions from both sides of the House, the Prime Minister said that the British and American Governments were in full agreement with the government of Israel concerning the entire issue. In the interests of Israel's national security, as well as to safeguard private individuals whose lives could be at risk, it had been mutually decided that no official statement would be released concerning the death of Mr Erter." What the hell do you make of that?'

'It's obvious—we're on to one hell of a story. If we can break it.' Cameron switched off the viewer and pushed his glasses up his nose, vigorously. 'Where do we start?'

'That woman, Kollek, sounds promising. Did you read about her?'

'Judith Kollek. Helped him found his Peace Party.'

'Yes.'

'But I don't think she was there when he was killed. I didn't find any mention of her being at the conference at all.' He lit his pipe. Wood, who loathed the smell of it, sighed.

'What about your lunchtime friend? He may know quite a bit more.'

'Mr John Merrion. No, I don't think so. It was just an idle remark to stop me pestering him about the airlines. He was living in Hong Kong when it happened anyway. I think we ought to go for this chap, Lathan.'

'Off-duty Lathan.'

'He's our only real lead—I wonder if he survived.'

5

There were times when Steve Lathan himself wondered if he had survived. This was one of them. The headache had hit him right in the middle of a meeting with Monsieur Rochet and sent him reeling; he could remember very little that Monsieur Rochet had said during the last ten minutes of their conversation. Not that this mattered greatly, for though the name of the firm, Lagarde et Rochet, was written in vast letters against the sky above the factory, it was in fact controlled by Quigley Components, Inc. of Cleveland, Ohio, and Lathan's real boss was one Stuart Loomis, Managing Director of what was euphemistically known as 'the joint Board'.

There were a lot of euphemisms bustling around Lagarde et Rochet, not the least enjoyable being the name of Steve Lathan's own department: '*Départment de la Paix Industrielle*'. He and Holly had many private jokes about Industrial Peace, and it did indeed encompass just about everything from trying to discover who had impregnated feeble-minded Anne-Marie of the cafeteria to infiltrating the more dangerous Communist cells on the factory floor and incapacitating them, by force if necessary. Holly maintained that her husband commanded more corrupt Corsican *flics* than the Minister himself: not quantitatively correct but qualitatively near the mark.

He had never told his wife about the headaches; she thought that he suffered from occasional migraines. What he really suffered from was the result of that blow on the head which had induced a hæmorrhage with an unpronounceable name. The bullet-wound gave him no trouble at all, but the hæmorrhage had nearly killed him at the time and had been making his life hell, on and off, ever since. Right now it was on.

He locked the door of his office, took the telephone from his desk, put it on the floor and lay down beside it. Ten, fifteen minutes' peace and the pain would begin to abate; at least he'd be able to grasp what people were saying and trundle out automatic replies; if he was granted twenty minutes, or even a merciful half-hour, he would be back to normal. The telephone rang after five minutes.

'Lathan. *Oui, m'sieur, immédiatement.*' Some clunk in die-casting had managed to chop off a finger, and the whole shop was at a standstill, solidarity, etcetera. He struggled to his feet, wondering whether he was going to pass out and who would handle die-casting best. Marchand probably, he was good on the shopfloor, made the workers think he was one of them; as in politics, two-thirds of the job was acting.

A few minutes after he had dispatched Marchand, with a six-man undercover back-up in case there was trouble, the walls of the corridor began to cave in on him. There were no indoor plants in the entire department, he had seen to that, but here he was once again fighting off the cruel swords of Sanseveria and the succulent kisses of Ficus Elastica. He tried to get back to his office, but measured his length in the passage before he could do so. Young Dr Ramponneau, who was on duty, knew the case-history and didn't waste a minute, packing him off *toute suite* to the nearest hospital, St Pierre du Nord.

They gave him a shot before the brain-scan, something they didn't like doing because drugs tended to affect the readings, but preferable to his coming round during the scan and smashing up that extravagantly expensive piece of equipment, newly acquired. What with one thing and another he was comatose for quite a long time and thus unable to ask people to preserve his little secrets; so the first thing he saw with returning consciousness was Holly's dear face looking stricken. He said, 'I'm sorry, honey, it was only another thing for you to worry about.'

She told him it didn't matter; all that mattered was that

there was nothing seriously wrong. The hospital was keeping him for twenty-four hours' observation; then he'd be back at home; and yes—seeing the anxiety in his eyes—back at work too. Monsieur Rochet himself had paid a visit to ask how he was; he had been most concerned and had said that Lagarde et Rochet couldn't do without Steve Lathan; Industrial Peace had never been so harmonious. He had also asked her to tell her husband that die-casting had gone back to work without a murmur.

Lathan nodded and smiled, thinking all over again how lucky he was to have found this girl. He tightened his grip on her hand and felt her fingers respond. Nobody had ever told him that there could be such deep understanding between a man and a woman, both physical and mental, so that one never knew where one began and the other ended.

Like a great many soldiers and policemen and others who volunteer for the thankless task of trying to maintain law and order in a lawless and disordered world, his personality was divided; there was a professional man and a private man. The professional was hard, calculating, capable of violence; the private man was really a very simple kind of person with a simple philosophy derived from his youth on a Kansas farm: Bible-belt discipline, decency, loyalty, plain country pleasures. He had vaguely imagined that one day he might marry, most people did; but he had never dreamed that there was a far more sensitive, not to mention sensual, Steve Lathan lying dormant inside him, waiting to be aroused by this woman, this one woman whose hand he now held in complete trust, complete accord, a silence stronger than words.

His wife kept the words until later, until they were having dinner at the table in their kitchen. The chill rain of this unbending April pattered at the window. The Comte and Comtesse de la Grande-Poitrine had had a row, and she had locked him out of the apartment. He was a dashing gentleman, a bus-driver, younger than his wife and perhaps half her weight, who never failed to give pretty Madame Lathan the eye when they passed in the street; so one didn't have to look far for the cause of the argument. Now, in his bedroom slippers, he had sploshed across to the Café des Sports and was no doubt warning some young blood, waiting for his turn at the football machine, against marriage.

Holly watched her beloved Métro, windows flashing as it rumbled along the 'elevated', slowing down at the approach to Cambronne; then she said, 'You'll have to take things a bit easier, Steve.'

He shrugged. 'I never have. Why now?'

'Because you fell flat on your face.'

He refrained from enforcing his argument by telling her that it wasn't the first time. 'I'm thirty-six, I'm not taking to a wheelchair.'

'You know perfectly well the kind of thing I mean. Not so many morning press-ups, no more swimming a mile out to sea, no more of the famous repeat performances in bed.'

'We'll see about that.' Grinning wolfishly.

'Steve, I talked to the specialist, I *know*. All right, I'm not asking how it happened, but it certainly wasn't falling off your bike when you were a kid.'

She had felt the scar during one of their earlier moments of intimacy, not a time for lengthy explanations. 'Best I could think of off the top of my head.' He loved this kind of dreadful pun, but his wife did not smile. 'And you're going to take a holiday.'

'Sure, 14th June, already booked.'

'Now.'

'Can't be done. War might break out in Industrial Peace.'

'Monsieur Rochet himself said you ought to go away for at least a week, so did the doctors. It's no good making faces, Steve, I'm serious—you need protecting from yourself and I'm damn well going to protect you!'

Brave words. In fact, as Time was about to prove, she was the one in need of protection.

6

A good thing about the job was that though they were subject to the Features Editor, known as Attila the Hun, the kind of stories they wrote under the *Follow-Up* heading were always potentially explosive. This meant that the Editor himself liked to keep an eye on them; if he was going to be rapped over the knuckles by the proprietor, or by some enraged foreign Ambassador or Cabinet Minister, it was as well to know all the facts in advance. Alistair Williams looked like a massive version of Peter Lorre, same hooded eyes, same sweet but dangerous smile; his humour was often described as 'Puckish'; if so, he was Puck armed with a flick-knife and an evil line in false innocence.

Thus he started off this particular interview by saying, 'Yes, I think you're on to a good idea. Didn't at first, I must tell you—raving lunatics usually have a limited news value.'

Tom Wood blinked; he knew better than to say anything, but Williams was on to the blink like a stoat: 'Of course *you* think Isaac Erter was some kind of sainted guru.'

There were limits. Wood replied, 'I think he was an exceptional man who died for what he believed.'

'You ought to be wearing flowers in your hair like a freak from the Sixties.'

'For God's sake,' said Wood, riled as intended, 'we're all in favour of *peace*, aren't we?'

'Of course. But nobody ever, *ever* in the whole course of history, got peace by being open and honest and laying their cards on the table. Ergo, the man was an idealistic old fool.'

'I get it. Like me.'

'Like you, Undoubting Thomas. How did you come to

have green eyes, I wonder, they're supposed to denote a devious character.'

If Cameron thought he was going to escape by keeping quiet he was wrong. 'Why are *you* looking so smug?'

'I was wondering how long it would be before somebody brought up the idealist angle.'

'You agree with me?'

'Well, my subject was History . . .'

'Yes, yes, and you got a First. Do you agree?'

'I don't like snap judgements, I'd need to know a lot more about the man.' The mild brown eyes were innocent behind the lenses, but the criticism had been sharp enough. Alistair Williams didn't mind a bit of criticism from the young; showed they were alive and had their wits about them; neither did he mind Tom Wood's idealism or the anger aroused by his mockery of it: all grist to the mill of a good end-product. As an old newspaperman now in charge of the country's best Sunday newspaper, that was all he really cared about. He said, 'I think it's a good idea because about half our readers are like Undoubting Thomas here, and think Erter was a sainted guru who died in the cause of peace—so a few meaty revelations from you will have them jumping up and down and arguing with the other half who think he was a fool. And that's what sales are all about.' He sat back in his chair and eyed them with interest. 'But, just as important—it came to me in the bath this morning—old Isaac is going to split the little Wood-Cameron atom right down the middle, and the ensuing explosion should be sensational.'

Cameron said, 'Nothing's going to split us down the middle, we're doing too well as we are.'

Their Editor let out an incongruous cackle of laughter. 'Beautiful! That's exactly what I mean. On the one hand, a perfectly amoral opportunist . . .'

'I try to be pragmatic, that's all.' Huffily.

'Pragmatic!' crowded Alistair Williams, eyes glinting

within their pouches. And to Tom Wood, 'Hear that?'

'What's so funny? It's true.'

'That's one of the things I like about you two—chalk and cheese, but you're loyal to each other.'

Silence. Both young faces defensive.

'I'm not complaining, God forbid! I'd ascribe forty per cent of your success to the chalk-cheese principle. You—' a glinting glance at Wood—'this moral clown, shining knight in armour, all that clap-trap. And you—' Cameron— 'a sneaky young amoral opportun ... I *beg* your pardon—amoral pragmatist. That's why you're going to do something really good on Isaac Erter—he's got you both by the short hairs already!' He looked at them expectantly, turning on the charm which generally concealed a base motive. After a moment they both smiled; he was an old bastard but he was a first-rate Editor.

'Got any leads?'

'One possibility,' said Cameron, 'that's all. Fellow called Lathan who tried to save his life.'

'American,' added Wood. 'Some kind of security-man, we think. If he's not dead.'

'So how do you find him?'

'We've got a ... You may remember—a contact-man at the US Embassy.'

'Oh yes. He's pricey, isn't he? But Embassy people always are.' He made a note. 'Have you checked with Whitehall? Official Secrets Act? I don't think there's a D-notice.'

Cameron said, 'We talked to Marshall on the phone. There's no D-notice, but he's asking around. We're seeing him at eleven.'

Clive Marshall was a thin upright man in his middle forties with a military bearing and a military moustache and haircut to match: in piquant contrast to the slightly camp manner he adopted when dealing with young male members of the Press. Bets were frequently made in Fleet Street as to how long it would be before he was arrested in a public convenience. In fact, he had never been anywhere near the army, give or take the odd guardsman, but had spent his life scurrying mole-like about the dark passageways of government. There wasn't much he didn't know about what went on behind the doors which lined those passageways.

'No objections to Isaac Erter,' he said, 'not a dicky-bird. So if that's what turns you on, go ahead.'

'What,' asked Cameron cautiously, 'about all that hot air in the House of Commons—"mutual decision that no official statement should be released"?'

Marshall bridled. 'Well, you know how it is. Prime Ministers have to say *something* at Question Time.'

'Why wasn't the result of the Official Inquiry released?'

'How would *I* know?'

'You must,' said Wood, 'have a personal opinion.'

'The last time I voiced a personal opinion to one of your lot it turned up on page one next day under a banner headline.'

'That wasn't us. You know we'd never do that.'

Marshall eyed them cannily. 'If it's printed you'll get no more help from me. None. Ever.'

'It won't be printed.'

'Well, as Auntie Agatha Christie was forever asking us, who had most to gain from his death?'

Wood tried, 'All those gun-crazy psychopaths in the Israeli Government?'

'*What* government, duckie? There are more than two dozen parties in Israel, so everything's a coalition anyway. Put it another way, who had most to *lose* if he got peace?'

'Ah,' said Cameron, 'you favour the KGB theory.'

'And I'll tell you why. Syria and a lot of other travellers are only chums with Russia for one reason: aid, which means arms. If there's peace it would be the end of Ivan in that neck of the woods. Islam and Communism don't mix.'

'It's a point,' Cameron conceded.

'And it doesn't stop there. Who else stood to lose their shirt if Isaac Erter succeeded? *How* many billions does the United States Government spend per year on arms for Israel?'

'You mean,' said Wood, 'the US armament industry.'

'Yes indeed. And all their middlemen.'

'So . . .' Cameron counted on his fingers. 'We've got the Russian connection, the arms pedlars of the world and their middlemen, any kind of terrorist . . .'

'Just like an Agatha Christie houseparty, everyone a suspect.' Marshall giggled happily.

Wood said, 'You haven't mentioned the Israelis themselves.'

'All those moulting old hawks, a nasty dangerous lot! If I was you, researching Isaac Erter, and I'm awfully glad I'm not, I'd be ever so careful who was behind me—you're up against a very *rough* group of boys!'

Their contact in the United States Embassy was called Phil, no surname. They had found him, or he had found them, by what appeared to be chance, but with the Americans you could never be sure. They had gone to the office of National Reconnaissance to ask the Press Officer a few relatively harmless questions about the reported breakdown of a satellite. Harmless or not, the questions were not answered. However, they had been overheard by Phil who appeared to be delivering some document to a secretary; he followed them out to the elevators and, after a swift glance this way and that, said quietly, 'Maybe I can help you guys.'

He looked like an over-age and out-of-condition American football player. What his job was at the Embassy they never discovered; he gave the impression that he had access to various classified documents but that he didn't work for the CIA or any of its subsidiaries, nor for the National Reconnaissance Office, nor the NSA (National Security Agency), nor the FBI, all of which were represented to a greater or lesser degree in Grosvenor Square. The point was that, as far as they knew, nobody outside these organizations had any access to the kind of documents with which their contact seemed familiar; therefore he was highly suspect. Were they in fact getting classified information out of Phil, in return for hard cash, or was he getting information out of them, gratis, and using their cash to throw extravagant departmental parties?

He *said* that he needed money because he was paying alimony in Nebraska while at the same time supporting a girl and their mutual child in Ealing; they supposed that it didn't really matter whether this was true or not; the fact was that on the three occasions when they'd had recourse to him his information had been useful and as far as they knew correct. And if he was indeed monitoring their stories, in case they were about to step on the sensitive toes of the United States, there was no harm done, because, had that been their intention, they wouldn't have gone near him.

As regards Off-duty Lathan, Phil stared into his coffee for a time—they usually met at a café on the other side of Oxford Street. 'You sure he was one of ours?'

Cameron said, 'The only report we can find says he was. And info about him was given to the media by a spokesman from your Embassy in Rome.'

'Then he was something to do with The Company.'

At their first meeting, a year ago, they hadn't known that the CIA was called 'The Company' nor that its centres all over the world were called 'stations'. Phil had been astonished; didn't they even read spy stories? Now he nodded to himself and said, 'He'll be filed some place, I'll go check. Where can I find you guys in . . . better make it an hour and a half?'

They gave him the telephone number of the *Daily Telegraph* library, to which they were extending their research. Phil said, 'Call you,' and stood up to go.

As he left the place a man sitting in the corner with a cup

of coffee refolded his newspaper and in doing so took a good look at the American. It was the same pale and unremarkable man with a slight widow's peak who had been waiting for Mr John Merrion in a Mercedes not far from the Garrick Club. By the time the two journalists also departed he was once again hidden behind a screen of newsprint.

Being American, Phil called them on the dot ninety minutes later: from a public telephone, of course.

Lathan, John Steven, had belonged to a subsection of the CIA known as IS-F, Intelligence Security—Foreign . . .

This was a new one on Cameron and Wood, though their knowledge of such circles was improving all the time.

Phil told them that the simplest way to explain the function of IS-F was to say that it was the CIA's private police force, brought into being in order to protect the Intelligence departments and their agents, to act as a buffer between this élite and the rude world outside. The Rome Conference at which Issac Erter had died was a perfect example of the kind of duty it performed; the CIA itself would certainly have had a man or two hidden there, a member of the Press Corps perhaps, or even one of the delegates, but it wouldn't have dreamed of showing itself overtly around the Hotel Imperia or in the streets of Rome. That's what Intelligence Security was for.

To return to Lathan, John Steven. He had been badly wounded trying to save Erter's life. Hospitalized for six months. Returned to duty in London with commendation for bravery. Met an English girl, Olivia Osborne, and decided to marry her. Girl judged to be SR . . .

Judged to be what?

SR, Security Risk. No reason given, only the reference number of a more secret document to which Phil did not have access. Lathan had to choose between marrying her and keeping his job. He chose marriage. The Agency respected his decision (commendation for bravery, etc.), helped him get a suitable job with a Franco-American engineering firm, Lagarde et Rochet, at Sannois, north-west of Paris. Lathan's present address, Flat 4, 27 Rue Mannin, Paris 5.

Phil had delivered again.

7

Thus far the initial phase of their search for the truth about Isaac Erter's death had proceeded in an orderly if unspectacular manner. Now all this began to change, but so subtly that at first nothing was noticeable.

When Tom Wood got back to his riverside flat, he found a disconsolate auburn-headed figure sitting at the top of the stairs. Henrietta. Only at the very moment of seeing her did he remember that somewhere on the other side of their Editor's barbed asperities, and Mr Marshall of Whitehall, and Phil the American conundrum, and more wearying, eye-boggling hours searching unsuccessfully for another lead in the *Daily Telegraph* library, he had indeed asked her to have dinner with him.

'Oh God!' she said, 'and I thought I *meant* something in your life.' She had a nice line in self-mockery. As he admitted her to the flat she added, 'And let me tell you, I haven't dressed up like this to be whisked smartly through a MacDonald's!'

She had indeed made herself look most delectable. Now that Wood examined her more carefully, and soberly, he saw that she really was very young; the make-up, the scent, the sophisticated dress, only emphasized a kind of leggy gracelessness which was in itself almost graceful; and inevitably touching. Examining her, kissing her lightly, Wood said, 'I've been cradle-snatching. Not really my line.'

'You didn't have any complaints, not that I noticed.'

'None. And thank you for cleaning the joint.'

'I'm a good cleaner, aren't I?'

He wished he could remember what she had told him about her job. Presumably she could see the void behind his eyes, he wasn't very good at hiding his thoughts. She said, 'Aggie Phipps, remember? I sell the clothes but I wear them as well, so I'm a kind of model. My goodness, you *were* pissed. I must say you carried it off jolly well.'

'Thanks. What'll you drink?'

'B and S—isn't that *smart*? My granny used to call it B and S, and now it's back.'

He mixed her a brandy and soda and gave himself a slug of Scotch. He was glad now that he'd made a date with her; she was a sexy and spirited little piece, and it would provide a nice ending to a successful week. (He and Cameron had already booked their flight to Paris for Monday morning.) He said, 'Look at the etchings or play the music or whatever while I take a quick shower. You know where the booze is.'

'Where will you feed me? I didn't have any lunch, I could eat a horse.'

'How about Etienne?'

'I adore Etienne. Can I have those fish-ball things in the shrimp sauce?'

'Quenelles. Yes.'

'Goody.'

When she heard him turn on the shower she went quickly to his document-case which he had thrown on to the big deal table. It wasn't locked; he wasn't the kind of man who would bother with locks; didn't have that kind of job anyway. She opened it quietly—no sound so unmistakable as the snap of catches on a document-case—and looked quickly through his notes which were gathered in a dog-eared blue folder. She found the name Lathan without much difficulty; and in one of the open pockets of the back flap she spied an Air France ticket, two Air France tickets: Paris return, outward flight on Monday at 9.30 a.m., return section open. Bit of a bonus that, she hadn't expected the tickets.

A critical observer, a critical opener of other people's document-cases, might have thought that she returned the notes to the blue folder rather untidily and not in their correct order; also that she made the mistake of returning the airline tickets back to front. She closed the case as silently as she had opened it, returned it to its former position, and went to mix herself another drink. The whole thing had taken no more than a couple of minutes. Tom Wood was still splashing about under the shower.

David Cameron's experience was of a somewhat more immediate nature. One of the reasons he and Shirley had decided on the modern Georgian house in Holland Park, despite its alarming price, was that at the end of the row of twelve were twelve garages in a small yard. Garages being as rare as rubies in any London residential street, and car-thieves being as common as lamp-posts, the garage was a considerable inducement to buy.

Cameron ducked out of his BMW into semi-darkness and pouring rain, unlocked the cantilevered door, pulled it up, ducked back into the car and drove it into dry seclusion, headlights illuminating Lucy's fairy-cycle, a pram, several deckchairs and other appurtenances of the summer garden. He switched off the lights, got out of the car, and at the same moment realized, with a tingling of the spine, that the cantilevered door was closing, was already half-closed. He caught a glimpse of the man who was pulling on it, a silhouette against the radiance of the street beyond. Then a clang, and total darkness.

Cameron had not turned on the garage light in advance, as he usually did, for what now seemed the most trivial of reasons; he hadn't wanted to get any wetter than he already was. So now he was trapped. With whom, for what reason?

A powerful flashlight, more like a searchlight, glared into

his face, pinning him against the deckchairs, and a deep voice said, 'Good evening, Mr Cameron. Please don't move, then you won't get hurt.'

Impossible not to recall what whimsical Mr Clive Marshall had said that morning: 'If I was you I'd be ever so careful who was behind me—you're up against a very *rough* group of boys!'

Tom Wood's evening began to fall apart visibly after Henrietta had finished a mountain of that delicious pudding which the French aptly call Mont Blanc: vanilla ice-cream buried in crème Chantilly and hot black chocolate sauce. She had preceded this with the favourite quenelles and a large veal chop cooked with herbs. Wood was waiting, fascinated, to see if she was going to top it all off with a nice big helping of assorted cheeses. Accompanied by a glass of port?

However, the pretty little face, when raised from a scoured dessert-plate, looked curiously doubtful; perhaps she was going to be sick. This suspicion became a virtual certainty when she excused herself with a wan smile and retired to the Ladies Room where she remained for a very long time.

Wood was just beginning to wonder whether she had, for reasons of her own, slipped out of the restaurant by a back door when she returned, looking pale but composed, and sat down with another wan smile.

'Oh God,' she said, 'if that isn't the pits!'

'What?'

She put out a soft childish hand and laid it over his paw. 'What *are* you going to think? Forcing you to bring me here, and eating all that, and now . . .' Leaning closer: 'I'm not due for at least a week, or I shouldn't be. Oh Tom, I am sorry, isn't nature *brutal?*'

So that was that. Wood had packed her into a taxi, it was still pouring with rain, and now, at ten-thirty in the evening, found himself standing outside Etienne with a vacuum where there should have been a climax. Moreover, the restaurant's doorman was giving him that certain look which would result, at any second, in some asinine suggestion as to where Wood could find himself a girl, or even what London chose to call a nightclub. He swung away angrily as the man took a step towards him and then realized, too late, that his only chance of getting another taxi on a night like this was to have waited until the doorman, using his own particular brand of bribery and corruption, plucked one out of the darkness.

Within a minute he was thoroughly wet, within two minutes soaked to the skin. Not at all the way he had visualized the evening's end.

But as it happened it was by no means the end, for as soon as he opened the door which admitted him to his converted warehouse he smelled Cameron's disgusting pipe, and upon reaching the top of the stairs found, for the second time that night, a shadowy figure waiting for him. They went into the flat, where he thrust a tumbler into his partner's hand, told him to help himself, and began to take off his dripping clothes.

Cameron, looking more than ever like an owl-eyed young professor, followed him around as he did so, describing the scene in the garage and repeatedly pushing his glasses on to the bridge of his nose.

'Who was he working for?'

'I couldn't make out. I thought at first he was an Israeli, but I don't think he was. Kind of a . . . cockney accent, I suppose.'

'That doesn't mean a thing.'

'He *talked* a lot about the Israelis—told me we'd find ourselves barred if we ever tried to go there.'

'What did you say to that?'

'I said we had no intention of going there, but if we ever did we'd get in somehow. He said he didn't think so—didn't I know that Israeli Intelligence was the toughest and most efficient in the world? By that time I was pissed off. I said in my experience they were about as tough as a bunch of half-baked bagels, and as for efficiency, the Jewish people seemed to me to be efficient everywhere except Israel.'

'How did that go down?'

'Pretty well. He laughed.'

'You're right, he wasn't an Israeli.' Wood was now comfortably enfolded in a woolly dressing-gown. 'Then what?'

'Then he got down to the nitty-gritty. He said if we knew what was good for us we'd drop the whole idea of Isaac Erter, it was none of our business. He said, '"It's a hand-grenade, Mr Cameron, and someone's pulled out the pin. If I were you I'd throw it and run."'

'Nice turn of phrase!'

'I told him where he could put his bloody hand-grenade.'

'Wise?'

'I didn't have anything to lose, did I?'

'Fingernails, eyes, balls.'

'Not this time, it was a warning. What do you make of it, Tom?'

'Same as I've made of everything since a chance remark started me off—we're on to a great story, and the more people who don't want us to do it, the better it gets. I wish we were in Paris right now.'

'Talking of that, I haven't got my ticket—did you take it?'

Wood made a face. The pragmatist had a habit of mislaying essential objects: cameras, tickets, notes, on one never-to-be-forgotten occasion a passport. He went over to his document-case, opened it, and put out a hand towards the airline ticket which peeped from one of its shabby pockets. The hand paused in mid-air; he was frowning. Cameron said, 'Oh God, don't tell me I've lost it!'

Wood pulled at the edge of the visible ticket, revealing that there were two. 'No, it's here. David, I put them in the other way round.'

Cameron joined him at the table.

'Like this, facing me, I always do.' He opened the blue folder and looked at the top sheet of paper. 'And somebody's been through this lot.'

'Are you sure?'

'Absolutely. The last note I made was about Mrs Erter, the widow—remember? It was on top.' He searched the folder and found the note in question. 'This page was on top.'

'Messy job, putting them back wrong!'

'Think so? Could be a neat job.'

Cameron, looking up sharply, found the greenish eyes bright with excitement. 'You mean . . . this is *your* warning.'

8

The man who had introduced himself to Tom Wood at the Garrick Club as John Merrion, but whose real name was Anthony Markham, was at that moment sitting in the cocktail bar of the London Intercontinental enjoying an Armagnac: another dark and immaculate suit, another unexceptionable tie, shirt-cuffs exactly in place, grey hair trimmed that very morning. Opposite him, sipping a crème-de-menthe frappée, sat the pretty girl known to Tom Wood as Henrietta.

'You saw the name Lathan?'

She nodded. 'And the address in Paris.'

'Good.'

'And I . . . you know, rearranged things a bit. He'd have to be as pie-eyed as he was the other night not to notice.'

Markham thought for a moment; then glanced at his wristwatch. 'What time's their flight on Monday?'

'Nine-thirty. Morning.'

'Thank you. Now, if you'll excuse me, I have another appointment.'

He believed in the compartment principle. Even a cursory

examination of the criminal world revealed it at its most basic. A crook who operated alone was rarely caught. A crook who ignored the compartment principle and used accomplices and, which was worse, let them be known to each other, increased the danger of being caught in exact proportion to the number of people involved. Markham applied this simple rationale to his own not-so-different type of operation; only he knew how many people he employed or how many of them were in use at any one time.

Of course there were occasions when he needed more than a single assistant in a particular place, but the men or women who were then, of necessity, permitted to meet each other were carefully chosen for their discretion; if they lacked that virtue they were dismissed as soon as they had played their part.

Thus he left the girl, briefly known as 'Henrietta', to finish he crème-de-menthe in the bar of the Intercontinental and walked up the street to the bar of the Inn on the Park. Here, as arranged, he found a thickset, neatly-bearded young man perched on a stool drinking a Scotch. David Cameron would instantly have recognized him, by voice, as the stranger who had forced an encounter in his garage.

His name was Paul Benedict; he had been born and brought up in Whitechapel, and possessed most of the characteristics, good and bad, of the Jewish East-Ender. He had gone to Israel in his teens, fired with enthusiasm, and had returned in his twenties, disillusioned.

Anthony Markham listened to what he had to report about Cameron; then asked, 'What was his attitude?'

'Cocky. Scared but cocky.'

'Answered back?'

'Sure.'

'Not in any way put off?'

'Just the opposite, I'd say.'

'Great—it hardly ever fails. Benedict, some time within the next week I'll need you to fly to Tel Aviv.' He examined the strong, bearded features with a glint of amusement. 'How does that grab you?'

'Always delighted to visit the homeland.' Slight emphasis on the word 'visit'.

'You might contact one or two of your old friends there. We'll need help.'

'Like firearms?' The younger man's whole face lit up at this idea.

'And possibly a vehicle. If so, something tough—four-wheel-drive would be useful. I'll ring you from the States when I want you to move. Make sure that answering-machine's working properly.'

'Bloody thing!'

'You're paid enough, why don't you buy a new one?'

Benedict gave him a black, bright look (their eyes were much alike). One of his East End Jewish tendencies was an extreme disinclination to part with money, and Markham knew it.

He left the Inn on the Park and went across to the Dorchester. This part of London might have been created for the compartment principle. The man who was sitting at a corner table, well removed from other drinkers, was a Political Officer, FS4, at the United States Embassy. His name was Pollard: young, plump, balding, mainly remarkable for large gold-rimmed glasses which magnified his tiny grey eyes, causing them to dominate his entire face.

Markham refused a drink and said, 'Well?'

'You were right. Some guy on the third floor gave them Lathan's address.'

'Know his name?'

'Not yet, but I'm working on it. Looks to me as if they've been monitoring your boys for about a year now.'

'Any particular reason?'

'They write some touchy stuff—so it would be routine.'

'I don't call handing out Lathan's address routine.'

'Testing perhaps, they do a lot of that. Seeing whether

Lathan rises to the bait, whether he takes money—how much he tells them or doesn't tell them. Useful for future reference. Or they could be testing your journalists vis-à-vis the good old US of A. Friend or foe, or even Commie?'

Markham took a handful of peanuts and ate them one by one. 'Do you think The Company will tail them in Paris?'

Pollard shook his head. 'If they tail anybody it'll be Lathan, he's the important one.'

'And if my boys go to Israel?'

'Yeah, well . . . that's a different fish-fry. *Then* I think they might move. Or hand it to the Israelis. Or both.'

Markham nodded. He didn't in the least like the idea of Wood and Cameron having access to information which had not been processed by him; of which he himself might be ignorant, though that was unlikely. 'What's the official attitude towards Isaac Erter having been killed by the KGB?'

'Firm favourite, always is. Anything awkward or inexplicable, or anything nobody *wants* explained. So . . . sure, the Russians killed Erter, why not? Sounds good.'

Anthony Markham considered this in silence, chewing the last peanut. Then: 'Find out the name of their Embassy contact, uh?'

'Sure. But slowly-slowly or the monkey catches me, right?'

'Right.'

'It might be clever to say nothing, just leave him there. Always useful to have a leak on hand, that's my theory. I mean, whoever he is, your two journalists trust him.'

Markham was far from sure how much he himself trusted Mr Political Officer Pollard. The hugely magnified eyes were too restless; he would do well to remove those all-revealing glasses on certain occasions. Also, whichever way you sliced it, he was at this very moment being a traitor to his government, a charge which could not be levelled at Markham himself since he wasn't employed by that government. As for this phoney leak in the plumbing of the CIA's London station, it might well prove useful at some future date. Leaks had a way of flooding the bathroom, sometimes the whole house. He said, 'Thanks, I'll be in touch,' stood up and left the bar.

In the lobby he paused, thinking. By Washington time it was now four o'clock in the afternoon. He didn't in the least want to put through a call, but could not evade the fact that it was professionally correct to do so. Sometimes he felt that professional rectitude was nothing but an albatross strung around his neck. He sighed, and made his way to one of the Dorchester's public telephones.

Eventually a dulcet secretarial voice said, 'Yes, London, we will accept the charges.'

'You're through.'

Markham said, 'Is Mr Braunsweg there? May I speak to him?'

'I'll inquire.'

Some fault in the office switchboard enabled him to hear a tiny replica of her inquiry and of Braunsweg's voice calling her rude names. What an unmannerly slob he was! He came on the line. 'Yes?'

'Just a small point.'

'If it's small why bother me?'

'The Embassy here has direct contact with our two men. It's been going on for a year. They know all movements to date. Are you with me?'

'I'm not an idiot.'

'This means that information will be passed upwards. You may need to stop it at your end.'

'Okay, I'll stop it.'

'You're sure? It could be critical.'

'You deaf or something? I said I'd stop it.'

'Because I can't do anything here. Which won't make any difference to the conclusion.'

'Jesus, I should hope not!' A faint snicker of malicious mirth. 'Have to work that little bit harder, won't you?'

'Not necessarily.' It gave Markham great satisfaction to replace the receiver at the very moment when the man in Washington was drawing breath for a further superfluous and probably boorish comment. He had acted professionally, the only thing that mattered.

He left the Dorchester and walked back along Park Lane to the Hilton. He found that he was smiling, and admitted to himself that so far things were going smoothly, apart from that loose end of the uncontrollable Embassy contact.

He also admitted to himself, now that the ploy had proved successful, that his initial move had been an unforgivable gamble. If Tom Wood had not risen to the bait ... Of course there were many other journalists in many other European countries, but this pair were not only the best, they fitted the role to perfection, and the loss of them would have been a professional wound. For a man who never gambled and seldom took risks that vital moment in the Garrick Club had been deeply disturbing; it must on no account, under any circumstance, be repeated. A word too little and Wood's interest might never have been aroused, a word too much and he might have become suspicious.

Luck, he thought, consciously denying the amount of forethought and experience which had enabled him to insert the idea of Isaac Erter into the young man's mind without once mentioning his name. As for the old trick of pretending to scare them off in order to strengthen their determination, he had never known it to miscarry.

And so, smiling, he entered the Hilton. It took him a little while to find what he was looking for, so perfect was the camouflage. As usual. The pale and unremarkable man with the widow's peak, who had followed Tom Wood from El Vino to the Garrick Club, as well as to and from some hundred other destinations during the past weeks, was sitting on a sofa in the lobby reading a paperback.

As he approached, Markham noticed that the title of the book was *Murder with Nine Motives*, which made him smile again; but he was also thinking that this really was the quintessential man for the job. Put him in London, Chicago, Paris, Cairo—no doubt in Vladivostock too, although it hadn't been tried—and he was instantly acceptable, accepted, forgotten. He never seemed out of place, and nobody gave him a second glance, and this in spite of looks which were in their own way striking. It had to be a kind of genius.

'Tennison—good evening.'

'Good evening, Mr Markham.' He put the book aside: face downwards, Markham observed with further concealed amusement.

'They're flying Air France. Nine-thirty on Monday morning. So you can go earlier or later, as you wish.'

'Earlier, I think.'

'Apparently they always stay at the Hotel de la Tour. I don't know it, do you?'

'Yes. First Arrondissement, not far from the Opéra. Good, quiet, no restaurant, no frills.' Tennison was half-French; his mother came from Bayeux.

'Problems from your point of view?'

'None I can anticipate. I'll stay there too.'

'You've got my itinerary?'

The man called Tennison produced a small black notebook from the inside breast-pocket of his unremarkable suit, and flicked past pages of numbers in groups of five: the names and addresses which any businessman carries around in a small black book, though not usually in cipher. 'Leave tomorrow, April 9th. 10th and 11th Washington. 12th New York. 13th to 17th Santa Barbara, if possible.'

'It won't be possible, I'm afraid.' And in the same breath, 'They have an independent source of information at the US Embassy.'

Tennison nodded. 'That must be the one they met for coffee this morning.'

'I'm afraid so. He gave them Lathan's address in Paris.'

Tennison's eyebrows raised themselves slightly.

'Exactly—my own reaction.'

'You think they'll tail them?'

'Them or him, I'm not sure. Certainly they mean to take some kind of action or why give them the address?' A quick glance, black and penetrating. 'Either way you'll have to keep a low profile, and I mean very. We're not taking on the whole CIA.'

Tennison nodded again.

'We have to wait and watch—until the fifty-ninth second of the eleventh hour, if you follow me.'

'Yes, I think so.'

'That way any move we're forced to make will have maximum impact.'

There was a pause. Markham leaned forward and looked at his hands, brown, capable, not quite as smooth as the rest of the physical façade. He said, 'We've got to break a link, do you understand? Somehow, somewhere, it *must* be done. Or they'll get ahead of me and I'll never catch up.'

The other man's silence contained a question.

'I'm talking about Israel. I must be in Israel before they are. I need half a day at least, a day would be preferable. We can only gain that kind of time by breaking the continuity.'

'Yes, I see.'

'Which means you. In Paris. If a chance doesn't present itself you'll have to create one.'

Tennison raised his eyebrows again and grimaced very slightly.

'No, it won't be easy. But I wouldn't demand it of you if I didn't think it was possible.'

'Well,' said Tennison drily, 'you could say I'm faithful, so all things are supposed to be possible. Then what?'

'Check with me. At once. That's why my dates are important. There may be a flaw, and I'm the only person who can see the whole picture.'

Tennison permitted himself a tight smile. In all the years he had worked for Markham only one person, Markham, had ever been able to see the whole picture; in Tennison's opinion it was the reason for his unvarying success.

'I don't generally make personal comments, you know that.'

Tennison knew that he never made personal comments; and if he was going to do so now it could only mean that he wanted to emphasize the importance of breaking a link and thereby extending time. Even so, the comment when it came was unique: 'This matter is important. It has worldwide implications.'

'Important' and 'worldwide' were strong and seldom-used words in the Markham vocabulary. What followed would have been excessive had it been spoken with any trace of feeling, which it wasn't: 'They think they have power, but we're the ones who make them and break them.'

Part Two

PARIS

'If you get your story you're going to end up accusing a *government* of murder, and that ain't peanuts.'

1

The telephone rang, as it often did, the moment Holly Lathan started cooking; she had just put some onions on to brown, whole small ones which needed constant turning. She took them off the heat, went into the living-room, turned down Mozart from the record-player, lifted the receiver. She expected to hear Steve announcing that he was going to be late for dinner that evening, delayed by some eccentricity of Industrial Peace, but it was a very English voice, precise and pleasant, with a trace of some North Country or Midland accent. 'Oh. This must be Mrs Lathan.'

'Yes, it is.'

'My name's David Cameron. I don't know if you read any of the British Sunday papers but we, my partner Tom Wood and myself, we write a feature called *Follow-Up* in the . . .'

She heard her voice saying, 'Yes, of course, I often read it, it's very interesting.' The voice sounded remarkably calm and rational, yet it seemed to her that the whole room had slanted sideways, the whole city, planet perhaps; she wondered if her thudding heart could be heard on the other end of the line. This was something she had dreaded long ago when the very sound of a ringing telephone had automatically evoked an uncontrollable spurt of fear. But long ago, long ago, almost forgotten. She should have known that such fears must never be forgotten and do not abide by the rules of time.

'. . . and we think your husband could help us. Any chance of a word with him?'

'He's not here at the moment,' replied the rational voice which didn't belong to her. 'Could you hang on a minute, I've got something on the cooker?'

She went slowly to the kitchen; turned off the heat; stood staring at the onions in their pan. Once her brain had been ready-primed with all manner of excuses and evasions; she must, she *must* pull herself together and drag some of them out of the dusty attics of her memory. They wanted to talk to Steve, not to her, yet what kind of reprieve was that? Anything to do with him involved her also.

She thanked God that this was her day off from Golden Promotions. It wasn't yet noon, which gave her a good six hours before he came home from work. What did they want? What *could* they want?

Back to the telephone, more purposefully. The room had regained its equilibrium and so to a certain extent had she; the backs of her knees were trembling, but at least they were made out of muscle and not aspic. She said, 'Sorry about that, it was rather complicated.'

'I hope I'm not spoiling anything. My wife's a super cook, I know how it goes.'

'Not at all. Mr Cameron, my husband hasn't been well. It's . . . Frankly, it's not something I can really explain over the phone. Could we meet and talk about it?'

'Yes, of course. We can come over . . .'

'No.' Much too sharp, but that couldn't be helped. 'No, I've got to go out anyway. Why don't we . . . ? Where are you now?'

'Near the Opéra.'

'Do you know the Café Villon? Corner of the Avenue and the Rue St Roch.'

'Yes, I think I do. Anyway, we'll find it.'

'In three-quarters of an hour.'

'Great. How will we know you?'

'I've got dark hair. I'll be wearing . . . a sort of snuff-coloured coat with a fur collar.'

'Fine. See you.'

It was by no means fine, merely the best she could contrive on the spur of the moment. A lot would now depend on what kind of men they were: on what kind of woman she was herself, come to that.

Mutual recognition was immediate; mutual appraisal instantly followed. They looked younger than she had expected; they had that particularly British, doggy friendliness which seemed so sincere and could be so misleading. The big one, to whom she had not spoken on the phone, Tom Wood, was what her mother would call 'a gentleman', but that was no criterion, and she doubted whether it ever had been; however, it meant that they came from roughly the same social background, which always made things easier. He was assessing her with the eye of a practised womanizer, but his charm was unforced, natural. The curly-haired one, with that trace of a Midland accent, was the more supple and devious character, the one to be watched; she knew this beyond doubt, instinctively.

For their part the two young men were surprised by her beauty and her chic. She had taken pains and had not spent four years in Paris for nothing.

The Villon was reasonably exclusive, daily lunch-time haunt of young executives and the smarter secretaries; in a few minutes it would be packed. She asked for a cognac, needed it, and waited; they weren't getting any leads out of *her*.

'We're planning to do a story about Isaac Erter . . .'

Isaac Erter! Oh dear God! Her heart sank into the murky waters of the past, and for a few seconds she couldn't even hear what they were saying. She had always in her deepest fears known that one day this would happen. Her instinct was to lie, but she couldn't begin to guess how much they already knew; possibly a good deal, that was their job. 'Isaac Erter. Yes . . . Yes, my husband was . . . involved in all that. Before I knew him.'

'We understand he tried to save Erter's life and was badly wounded—would that have anything to do with his present . . . ?'

'Yes. Please don't think I'm being obstructive, but you see he has . . . recurring symptoms. He only came out of hospital on Friday. If you start asking questions . . . And on that particular subject.' Her distress was very real, and she was pleased to see that they were perturbed and embarrassed by it. 'Surely . . . Surely there must be other people who can tell you about Erter?'

'The fact is—' truthful Wood began, but was cut short by his partner: 'Yes, I'm sure there are. If you could fill us in a little on the background . . .'

Tom Wood saw the dawning of a gleam of hope somewhere behind her eyes. He thought, not for the first time, that Cameron was a right bastard, but a clever one.

'Yes, of course. Ask *me* anything you like.'

Cameron came back with a straight left to the jaw: 'Why on earth did the CIA think you, of all people, were a Security Risk?'

She took the blow like a hardened fighter, looking him straight in the eye; then, glancing down at her brandy: 'I see you know all about it, but I suppose you would. I mean, you couldn't write such good articles if you didn't poke and pry into other people's business.' The change of attitude, borne out by the change of tone, was plain. Tom Wood gave Cameron a look which meant that he thought Cameron had overplayed the part. Cameron may have agreed, because he let his partner take over; on the other hand, he may simply have thought that it was politic to follow a potential knock-out blow with a little gentlemanly *politesse* which was not his line. 'Personally,' Wood said, 'I wouldn't have thought the Security Risk angle had anything to do with it.'

'It has. In a way.' She pushed back the collar of the coat, revealing a very nice neck; she watched Wood admiring it. Fascinating eyes; green was unusual in men. 'All right—if you're interested. It's all quite straightforward, a bit silly. Steve and I fell in love when he was working in London. He told me he had to report our relationship to his department.

I must say I rather resented that, but ... Anyway, they checked me out and decided that I came up to their immaculate standards.' Her smile was ironical. 'Then something happened which proved they had a point—weren't quite as daft as I thought they were.' She sipped her cognac and was glad of its fiery warmth sliding down into her leaden stomach. 'I'd known him for about ... oh, four months, we'd decided to get married. This woman came up to me at a party and started paying me ... clumsy compliments. Frankly, I thought she must be a lesbian. Not a bit of it. She suggested, she actually had the gall to suggest, that I might like to supply her with information about what Steve was doing, what jobs he was engaged on—in return for cash, I ask you! Those people must be ... backward!'

'Those people?' echoed Wood. 'Russian?'

'Something of the sort, obviously. I didn't wait to find out. I told Steve at once and he passed it straight to his boss. We couldn't have been more open and honest, either of us.' She spread her hands. 'Security Risk!'

Cameron shrugged. 'It doesn't take much. Often not that much.'

'But they'd already checked me out and given me an absolutely clean sheet.'

Wood said, 'I'm afraid it's a fact of life in those circles, they've had their pinkies burned too often.'

She sighed. 'So suddenly it was a matter of Steve deciding whether he wanted me or the job, and he ... I think he really loved his work. He's quite a simple man in lots of ways—he felt he was doing something for America.'

'But he chose you.' The tone was appreciative. She had to admit that he was attractive.

Cameron came back into the ring, punching. '*You* don't want us to talk to your husband, you're afraid it might aggravate his ... his condition, but does *he* think that?' The brown eyes were regarding her frankly, earnestly. She had a theory that it was dangerous to trust people with brown eyes, there was a warmth in them which was often misleading. She herself had brown eyes. 'I mean, isn't it possible that he might *like* to talk to us, maybe get it all out of his system?'

The question brought her face to face with herself, sharply; not a very pleasant encounter. The two young men were watching her with interest. She must answer, yet she was unable to answer. Gaining time, she said, 'I'm not sure. He was very ill—I couldn't bear it to happen again. He looks so strong, but sometimes . . .'

The big one who liked women came to her aid, gently courteous. 'Why don't you . . . feel him out? David could be right.'

'Let's make a deal,' said Cameron, who evidently liked deals, the eyes behind the horn-rimmed glasses were shining. 'We'll hold off until you've talked it over with him, how's that?' He didn't say, didn't need to say, what he intended to do then. It wasn't a deal at all, it was merely a stay of execution.

Wood gave his colleague an impatient, almost an angry, glance. 'Look—it was very nice of you to meet us, and be so frank with us. You're quite a girl anyway, protecting him like this.'

He meant it; but she had a suspicion that the devious one had already guessed that she wasn't protecting Steve at all, she was protecting herself.

2

The man whom Anthony Markham called Tennison had arrived in Paris by the first plane from London, so that he was already installed in Room 43 at the Hotel de la Tour when Wood and Cameron registered at Reception. The lobby was small; he had no difficulty in hearing that they had been given their 'usual rooms', 57 and 67, one above the other on the hotel's quietest corner.

Tennison himself, who spoke fluent colloquial French, thanks to his mother, was registered as Monsieur Victor Picon, a businessman from Grenoble. He had naturally foreseen that the two journalists would not share a room, and this had given him food for considered thought. Even taking into consideration the tiny size of modern equipment, the placing of two devices, one in each room, doubled the chance of discovery. Tennison took very few chances anyway and no double ones. In his experience, friends staying in the same hotel habitually met in one particular room, and he quite frankly ascertained beyond doubt which room Wood and Cameron would use; No. 67, Cameron's, was really a suite with a diminutive 'salon'.

Most unusually there was no convenient café opposite the hotel, so Tennison looked in shop-windows, fed pigeons, and spent a long time buying two magazines from a newspaper kiosk. It took the young men half an hour to settle in, unpack, make a few telephone calls. They left the hotel at eleven forty-five. Tennison knew that the receptionist with whom he had himself registered had gone off duty long ago, to be replaced by another young girl. He judged that twenty minutes would be enough to blunt her memory, and he guessed that she would either be painting her fingernails under cover of the desk, or telephoning a boyfriend, or flirting with the Assistant Manager who was also, he deduced, the owner's son.

She was, in fact, telephoning a girlfriend: 'He didn't! My God, what did you do?' Tennison said briskly, 'Room 67, please?' She handed him the key without hesitation, at the same time saying, 'Well, it's up to you. *I* wouldn't put up with that sort of thing for five minutes . . .'

There was really no need for Tennison even to leave the lobby in order to take an impression of the key; indeed he hardly did so, and was back at the desk, looking confused, in less than a minute: 'I'm so sorry, I must be mad—why did I ask for 67, I'm in 43?' This produced the vaguest of smiles and the correct key. 'No, I wouldn't go that far, but you could ring him and tell him you don't feel well . . .'

For the sake of appearances Tennison spent a few minutes in his own room; then left the hotel and went to a small side-street near the Gare St Lazare where Monsieur Lamartine, an old friend, cut the key for him there and then. It was possible that he could have done without it since he foresaw only two visits to Cameron's room and could easily, by the look of it, have used the real key without anyone noticing. This method, however, was safer.

By now it was 12.30, not an hour at which visitors to foreign cities were liable to return to their hotel: unless they proposed to lunch there, and the Hotel de la Tour had no restaurant. Tennison would have preferred to wait until 8.30 that evening, time of maximum safety, when all but the sick and a few Americans who liked to eat early (and paid for it by being given terrible food) were having dinner; but something told him that on this particular occasion speed was important; a lot could happen before evening and he needed to know about it.

So he waited until 1.30. Two young men who had made an early start to the day would certainly be assuaging their hunger by then; what was more, the hotel maids would have paused in their cleaning. As expected, the corridors were empty. As expected, Monsieur Lamartine's key worked perfectly. He had long ago decided where to plant the device: inside the base-plate of whichever standardized Hotel de la Tour lamp was nearest to the telephone. He had practised on the lamp in his own room and could carry out the whole operation in six minutes flat. Eight minutes later, an extra two for the descent by staircase, it was all over.

He opened his hanging-cupboard and took from behind the two grey suits and the drab raincoat what looked like an ordinary document-case; unlocked it and opened it to reveal a neat block of electronic equipment. He switched on the recorder, which would be automatically activated by the sound of a human voice in Room 67 (television, and to a lesser extent radio, played merry hell with it but didn't impair its efficiency), relocked the case, and then went out for his own luncheon.

David Cameron knew that his partner was angry and didn't approve of the way he had handled Steve Lathan's wife, but in his opinion certain situations and certain people demanded a little ruthlessness, otherwise nothing moved. In Wood's opinion the same results, or better, could have been obtained by more subtle means, without running the risk of antagonizing her. It wasn't the first time that this particular difference had divided them and it wouldn't be the last: as their Editor had said, 'chalk and cheese', and he had attributed forty per cent of their success to the fact. He had also said that Isaac Erter was going to split 'the little Wood-Cameron atom right down the middle', and they were both equally determined to prove him wrong.

For this reason Tom Wood was exercising unusual self-control: they were partners, they were intelligent and reasonable people, they were in pursuit of a very good story, possibly the best they'd ever undertaken. Yet the anger persisted, and in the course of their lunch the precise reason for it became plain to him. Needless to say, once he'd perceived it he found it lurking behind every sentence the other man uttered.

It seemed to be a day for remembering the words of their revered and acid Editor; what had he called Cameron? 'A sneaky young amoral opportunist.' All right, it was a harsh description but, Wood was inclined to think, a perfectly just one. And the issue which now divided them illustrated it to perfection: because what they were really bickering about over this elegant food in this elegant restaurant was the matter of how much right they, Cameron and Wood and others like them, had to intrude upon the private lives of private individuals. As far as Wood was concerned, no 'right' at all; as far as Cameron was concerned, a kind of Divine Right of the Media.

This discovery should have dissipated the anger, but it did no such thing. They were walking back to the hotel against a cold northerly wind when Cameron, glancing at his colleague's preoccupied face, said, 'Come *on*, Tom! You said yourself that the more people who didn't want us to do the story, the better you liked it.'

'True.'

'Well, now we've got another, haven't we? Pretty Mrs Lathan.'

Wood nodded. He intended to do no more, but somehow it didn't work out that way. He said, 'You don't care, do you? You honestly don't care if Lathan *is* ill.'

'Tom, he's the only lead we have.'

'And if we barge in on him and he . . . he has a nervous breakdown or something, that doesn't matter, the only thing that matters is the bloody story!'

They came into the lobby arguing. They argued across the reception desk and into the elevator. The doors closed on their argument, but it could still be heard ascending.

In Room 43 Tennison, who was lying on his bed with a good detective story, noticed that the voice-activated spool of the recorder had begun to rotate. He slipped off the bed and gently turned the Direct Volume control. Cameron was saying, '. . . course I agree with you, but we have no option.'

'She was afraid, couldn't you see that?'

'Yes, I saw it. And since we've got this far, I may as well say I wondered *why* she was afraid.'

'I'd have said that was bloody obvious. He's just come out of hospital, she thinks you'll go galumphing in and jump all over him, and bingo! he's back in hospital again.'

'I wonder.'

'God! you give *everyone* ulterior motives, don't you?'

'Yes. And nine times out of ten that's exactly what they've got.'

'I'm damn sure *she* hadn't.'

'How the hell can you be damn sure of any such thing? What's *your* idea, then? Come on, let's have it—let's have the Tom Wood alternative?'

An awkward silence. Then Wood's voice, highly defensive: 'If she comes back and says her husband won't . . . shouldn't talk to us . . .'

'Won't or shouldn't, which?'

'They come to the same thing.'

'Oh, for Christ's sake, Tom! Have you gone bananas, have you fallen in love with the bloody girl or something? "Won't" means he doesn't want to; "shouldn't" means she's persuaded him not to—and she will if she can. Either way, what do you do then? Drop the whole story?'

'Of course not.'

'For the hundredth time, Steve Lathan is our only lead. Whether he likes it or not, whether she likes it or not, we've *got* to talk to him—it's as simple as that.'

'And if she tries to stop us?'

'She already has, she'll try it again.'

'And?'

'We push her out of the way and we go ahead. There's no way she can prevent it.'

'That's another thing—you always underestimate people.'

A snort of irritation.

'If you upset her enough, and you probably have already, she might . . . remove him altogether—take him away on a holiday, why not? Then where would we be? Up the creek without a paddle.'

Tennison had listened gravely to this exchange, giving it all his attention. A few minutes later, when the conversation ended on Wood saying he was going out for a walk, and the spool stopped turning, Tennison leaned forward, switched off Direct Volume and sat for a long time staring at the machine.

'God! you give *everyone* ulterior motives, don't you?'

'Yes. And nine times out of ten that's exactly what they've got.'

3

Holly Lathan had always suspected that one day she would find herself trapped in this very web, spun by herself out of her own stupidity and indecision. As it happened, Wood had accurately judged her immediate reaction; she had gone straight from the Café Villon to Thomas Cook's in the Place Madeleine. If she could make it a *fait accompli*, tickets booked, hotel reserved, they could be in . . . Morocco by tomorrow evening or at the latest the day after. The doctors wanted him to take a holiday, Monsieur Rochet wanted him to take a holiday, what could be more simple?

But in the middle of her conversation with a very helpful young man, the idea and the hope had slowly ebbed away, leaving her floundering like a stranded fish; her voice unwound itself to a standstill and the helpful young man was left staring in bewilderment.

You didn't, you couldn't run away from a thing like this; the very act of running away would convince them that there was something to hide, whereas at the moment they were only motivated by ordinary professional interest. And, for God's sake, it wasn't the stupidity of Holly Lathan which interested them anyway, it was the assassination of Isaac Erter. She apologized to the helpful young man, left the travel agency, walked furiously in the cold north wind: across the Tuileries Gardens, and then to and fro, to and fro.

Yes, but the stupidity of Holly Lathan was inextricably *entangled* in the assassination of Isaac Erter, that was the point. One question could lead to another, and another and another, and what was to stop one of them leading to the cell in which she had imprisoned her wretched secret, flinging open the door, exposing it to the full glare of day? She could see the exact expression on Steve's face when he understood what she had done.

She came to a standstill, beating her gloved hands together in agony. She knew that passers-by were staring at her, a beautiful and agonized young woman in a smart coat, beating her fists together, just as this chill wind was beating the young chestnut leaves above her head. Being French they would think, 'Ah, the poor thing, her lover has left her, but she's young, she'll get over it.'

For God's sake, why hadn't she told him the truth long ago, at the time? But that would have been quite impossible. Then why hadn't she told him at some well-chosen moment during the ensuing years? Passionately she wished that the two damnable young men had never appeared (Isaac Erter, of all people, a ghost stretching out a dead hand to crush her); wished that the past hours could be sucked back into the maw of time, swallowed and never regurgitated.

When she opened the door of the flat and saw all the small, often shabby, objects which added up to her life with Steve and her love for him she could have burst into childish tears of grief and rage. She must think, *think*, find a way out, there was always a way out.

But she couldn't think. In growing panic she realized that the ability to form rational thoughts had deserted her utterly. Ideas churned around in her mind like odd pieces of clothing in the washing-machine, formless, unidentifiable, soaking wet. So great was her desolation that the telephone-call, when it came, that extraordinary and terrifying telephone-call, seemed almost like deliverance. No more panic, not even any choice, the choice whisked out of her hands and made for her. A man's voice: 'Madame Lathan?'

'*Oui.*'

'You prefer to speak in English or French?'

'I don't mind. Who are you?'

'English perhaps. As you'll see, there must be no misunderstanding. I take it your husband is not yet back from his work.'

'No. Who are you?'

'That isn't important.'

'It is to me. I don't talk to people who won't tell me their name.'

'Names, what do they matter? If I said my name was . . . Kollek, it would be meaningless.'

She froze for a long moment; then let out her breath in something between a gasp and a sigh; felt for a chair and sat down. After a time she said, 'I . . . I suppose you're something to do with . . . those two journalists.'

'They don't know me, they don't even know I exist. But what I have to say does concern them. Have you got over your surprise, are you listening carefully?'

'Yes.'

'For your own good, Mrs Lathan, I must ask you not to prevent them talking to your husband. If he's unwilling to see them you must encourage him to do so.'

'But how . . .?' She decided not to ask, but he voiced her thought anyway: 'How do I know you're trying to keep them apart? Again, that's not important.' It was like talking to God or to one's own conscience.

'And if I . . . refuse to do what you say?' She knew the answer because of that name which he had plucked out of the past, but also knew that she must hear it said.

'Then I shall tell your husband the truth. A few weeks after you'd met him in London, when you were already having an affair, you were approached by a woman called Judith Kollek and asked to spy on him because of his association with the death of Isaac Erter. Yes?'

She nodded. Then, realizing that he couldn't hear the nod, said, 'Yes.' No more than a whisper.

'For various reasons you agreed to do so.'

'They thought he might have actually killed Erter, they . . .'

'Yes, yes—we both know what they thought, and we both know that you agreed to spy on him, question him. Only *he* doesn't know it.'

She realized that she was weeping; fought against the tears savagely. 'That . . . That was before I was . . . in love with him. As soon as I realized, I told them, they released me.'

'Of course. As a girl in love you were useless. For reasons of guilt, one imagines, you then invented the story of being approached by an unknown woman, a foreign agent, possibly connected with the Eastern bloc. You were checked out, for the second time if I'm not wrong, and found to be clean. But they decided not to trust you anyway—they aren't all that clever in some respects, their reputation exceeds their claim to it. You're still there?'

'Yes.'

'The fact remains you spied on Lathan . . .'

'Please stop using that word.'

'You spied on him and you passed information to Judith Kollek—for nearly two months. Your husband would resent that deeply.'

'All right, all right—I'll do as you say, I won't . . . try to stop them talking to him.'

'I'm glad you're so reasonable.'

'What else?'

'Nothing else. It may seem only a small thing to you, but it's important. You understand?'

'Yes.'

'And if he's hesitant you'll encourage him to see them?'

'Yes.'

'Excellent. Au revoir, Madame . . .'

'Wait—please! If I do this, you won't . . .?'

'I shall tell your husband nothing, I can assure you of

that. I may use . . . dishonourable methods but I'm not a dishonourable man.' The statement had an odd kind of dignity, almost but not quite absurd. And it was true; Tennison was not a dishonourable man, he was merely a professional.

She replaced the receiver and sat there staring at it: or rather through it at herself aged nineteen. Olivia Osborne, that formless, feckless, subdivided creature, now seemed a complete stranger; she could hardly remember what the girl had thought about, apart from music which she was studying, and the things she had done seemed to have no connection with her thoughts anyway.

It was even difficult, now, to recall the impact Isaac Erter had made on her generation, but it had been profound. For quite a long time the famous photographic poster, in which Erter resembled a cross between Albert Einstein and the popular concept of Moses, had decorated bed-sitter walls once graced by Che Guevara, James Dean, David Bowie, and even less important gods.

In those days her friends had done a lot of marching about; trailing about would have described it better, for anything less like marching would have been hard to find. Any excuse seemed to suffice, but nuclear gadgets, whether warlike or peaceful, and cuts in student grants, and ecology in general, and sometimes the rights of other people like nurses or railwaymen, had all called forth processions of sympathetic trailers, chanting and smiling sheepishly and carrying illegible banners. The habit still persisted, she caught occasional glimpses of them on television. Olivia Osborne had thought it all a bit hypocritical, most of them didn't really care about these causes at all.

But Isaac Erter had been a different matter altogether; here was a man, a kind of grandfather-figure and therefore more lovable than a father-figure, who was standing up for peace in a context which really meant something; a man who had the guts to say what he thought of violence and war, and who was prepared to fight against them: a shining example of courage and integrity, towering above the muddle which was all that the world had to show its children for millenia of 'civilization'. Youth had flocked towards Isaac Erter, whatever their country of origin, and on this occasion Olivia Osborne had gone with them.

She had done more than this. In the company of a nice, earnest boy called Henry Something-or-other, studying the violin, she had actually visited the headquarters of IEPI, the Isaac Erter Peace Initiative (London) and had put her name down as an 'active supporter'. She wasn't quite sure what active support meant and, like thousands of others, would never have found out if chance had not intervened.

Who could he have been, the man on the phone? How could he have learned so much about her? Why was he so determined to ensure that her husband talked to the two journalists if, as he claimed, they didn't even know of his existence?

The murder of Isaac Erter had galvanized her generation into shocked activity; a real, heartfelt wave of horror had surged through them; they had rushed to and fro like disturbed ants, as energetically but, she now realized, to far less effect; for by the time she met Steve Lathan some six months later the assassination had been all but forgotten, sunk in a morass of other disasters, other causes.

From the beginning she had found Lathan overwhelmingly attractive, in spite of the fact that she didn't particularly like fair men and was unnerved by blue eyes. (She was still unnerved by them, by Steve's most of all when he so wished.) He was the only one of the three men she had known, in the biblical sense, who aroused her physically: with such violence that she was frightened, both of herself and of him. Yet she could not have walked away from him if she'd wanted to; and in a way she *had* wanted to, the strength of her passion was that alarming.

It was at this strange moment of her young life, when she truly didn't know whether she was coming or going, that she had found an unknown woman waiting for her one afternoon in the entrance hall of the Royal College of Music. Her name, she said, was Judith Kollek; she was an Israeli; she had been very close to Isaac Erter and had worked with him for ten years; she had helped him found his Peace Party and had been instrumental in making it the worldwide phenomenon which it had become. She knew that Olivia Osborne had enrolled as an 'active supporter' and she was now going to call upon that support.

The followers of Isaac Erter had not been satisfied with the official explanation, if it could be called an explanation, of his death, and they were determined to find out who was really responsible. It was thought that a certain American, an officer attached to a department of the CIA known as Intelligence Security, had himself killed Erter; and if he hadn't they were convinced he knew who had. His name was Steve Lathan. She understood that Olivia Osborne was . . . friendly with him.

Now, of course, it seemed insane that she hadn't immediately turned her back on this woman, on the whole idea. But at the time she wasn't in love with Steve, she was obsessed by him physically, and afraid: of him and of the obsession equally. It was even possible that in some ingenuous way she supposed that if he was guilty of so terrible an act, full knowledge of it, proof of it, would set her free from the thrilling and sickening roller-coaster-ride which was their relationship. Perhaps Judith Kollek had also made her feel exciting and important, a budding Mata Hari.

Oh God, it didn't matter now why she had agreed to question him, to report what she found out. The fact was that she had done it, and ironically, typically, the more she discovered about him, as a man rather than a demon-lover, the more she liked him. By the end of six weeks the metamorphosis had taken place, and the one thing she would have guaranteed to be impossible had happened: she had fallen in love with him.

By this time Judith Kollek was convinced of Steve Lathan's innocence; he was in fact, and as reported, a brave man who had tried to save Isaac Erter's life and who had nearly lost his own in the attempt. She smiled at the girl's confession, wished her good luck, thanked her for her assistance in clarifying the matter, and dispensed with her services.

It was at this point, there and then, that Olivia Osborne should have confessed the whole thing to her lover. What had stopped her was the intimidating knowledge that a part of him which she didn't know and was never going to know, inhabited another harsher world; people there might live by other, harsher standards; if she told him the truth he might give her a cold blue glare and walk out of her life forever.

But she had to do *something*, she had to absolve this terrible feeling of guilt. Poor little dim-witted creature! Presumably she had thought her solution very clever because it was reasonably close to the truth: that story, which she had repeated to the two young Englishmen, of being approached by a woman at a party, a woman who wanted her to report on Steve's professional activities, and of how she had so piously refused.

She couldn't see the trap. Her ignorance of his world was so complete that she didn't even know a trap existed. Thus, unwittingly, she had forced him into the appalling position of having to choose between his girl and his job. And he had chosen to give up the job. This was the crux. This was the Pandora's box upon which she must eternally sit lest the lid fly open and its contents destroy her. He might well laugh at the idea of her spying on him; he would not laugh at the stupid lie which had made him abandon an important career, one he had loved. For that, she suspected, as did the unknown man on the other end of the telephone, he would never forgive her.

'If he's unwilling to see them,' the voice had said, 'you must encourage him to do so. It may seem a very small thing but it's important.' Important to whom? And why? And why did she believe him when he said, 'They don't know me, they don't even know I exist'? The answer was an odd one: she believed him because he wasn't a liar; in every other respect what he had said was all too disastrously true.

When Steve Lathan got home he found her sitting at the kitchen table with a late cup of tea, staring out at their street; everything loose was swinging or fluttering in the wind. She tried to conceal what she was feeling, tried to give him the usual welcome, but he knew all her moods and had in any case undergone long and meticulous training in the art of recognizing prevarication. 'What's the matter?' he said. 'What's wrong?'

'Nothing.'

He stood there with a drink in his hand, eyeing her, frowning and smiling at the same time. She loved him very much when he did this; it seemed such an exact reflection of his character, serious but quick to laughter, happy-go-lucky in spite of every set-back: having to give up his chosen career, a blow on the head which had nearly killed him and now pursued him with malign complications.

'Come on, Holly, what is it?'

For some reason she still fought against telling him about the two Englishmen even though she had long since been defeated and knew she would have to tell him sooner or later. She flung herself into his arms, crying, 'I'm in a lousy mood, that's all. I feel *lousy*.'

So then they lay on the bed and made gentle love, while the wind moaned outside in the street and their dinner of Carbonnade Flamande, proper cold wind food, simmered in the oven. It should have been perfect, the two of them locked away with their love, safe from the cold uncaring world, but all she could think was, 'So much, so *much* to lose!'

However, as they lay together afterwards she did at least find it quite easy to tell him. He showed no surprise but said, after a while, '*Follow-Up*—we've read a couple of their things, haven't we? Not bad.'

'I wanted to keep them away from you, I don't want them upsetting you.'

'Hence the lousy mood.'

'Yes.'

He hugged her tightly. 'Takes more than a couple of journalists to upset me.'

'Yes, but . . . Isaac Erter.'

He grunted and was silent, withdrawing into the other world which was denied to her. Eventually he said, 'Better to play it straight with guys like that, honey. If you don't, they only invent things.'

During dinner he told her about his day: a farcical meeting of Shop Stewards, all knifing each other in the back while at the same time sententiously calling each other '*mon frère*'. Somehow 'my brother' sounded even worse than the English 'brother'. As always his quiet and humorous practicality calmed her; the fears and horrors of the day, even that telephone-call, receded. It was almost as if she was haunted by waking nightmares just as he was haunted by sleeping ones.

By the time they finished their meal he had already made up his mind; he discussed the decision with her because they always discussed decisions, but she doubted if he would have listened even if she had begged him on her knees not to talk to the two young men; as it was she could only adopt an attitude of pliant and wifely acceptance. But she did say, 'Steve, *why* are you going to see them?'

'I just told you.'

'No. Deep-down why?'

'Maybe,' he said, 'I want them to find out who hit me

over the head so I can slug them right back.' He dialled the number of the Hotel de la Tour.

4

They met for dinner the following evening, all four of them. Holly Lathan had not expected to be included, and was still struggling with the implications of that inclusion; it seemed to mark some major development in her relationship with her husband; for a few minutes he was going to open the door which led to his other life, and she was going to be allowed to look through it; in spite of years of curiosity, she was apprehensive of what she might see.

David Cameron and Tom Wood were also nursing uncertainties. Cameron was relieved that he had not been forced to put his strong words into action, pushing Mrs Lathan out of the way in order to reach her husband and their story. The prime reason for this relief was that such a course could only have antagonized Wood more strongly; in his partner's anger of the previous day he had sensed, for the first time, a threat to their working relationship and thus to their success; it was not a sensation he'd enjoyed. Wood, for his part, had also felt the earth shaking under their feet, and as the ostensible cause of the tremor he had enjoyed it even less; he was thankful that Steve Lathan had saved the situation, for the time being at least, by his willingness to talk to them. Each had therefore been gentle with the other, avoiding the 'I-told-you-so' which each felt he had a right to say.

As for Steve Lathan, his uncertainty was the most acute of all, because he strongly doubted the wisdom of what he was doing yet felt impelled to the doing of it. In answer to his wife's question he had said that he was going to meet the two journalists because he wanted to know who had hit him over the head so that he could hit them back; and this was true, though not on quite the simplistic level implied by the words.

He was, as she had said, a simple man, even though he had chosen to follow a devious career. He had genuinely admired Isaac Erter, so straightforward both in his aims and his philosophy, and this admiration was redoubled on closer acquaintance, brief but oddly intimate. In Rome, meeting him every morning, he soon became aware of the fact that Erter was ill, that the conference was taking its toll of him; twice he had asked for an arm, quietly so that no one else could hear, and the weight which he had put on it spoke for itself.

What he really wanted, then, was for the world at large to know the truth about the old man, not only about the manner of his death but about the courage and integrity which had been the cause of it: two virtues which the world at large conspicuously lacked. Moreover, he felt that he *owed* the truth to Erter, something else which the world at large might have had difficulty in understanding.

This gathering of uncertainties was watched by Tennison from a large and busy café almost opposite the chosen restaurant. He saw the two young Englishmen arrive, and disappear through the extravagant Art Nouveau doors; five minutes later the Lathans followed. Tennison resisted an inclination to join them and to dine at a nearby table. The odds on being remembered by one of four people were high enough, but when one of the four was Lathan they became suicidal. In any case he knew roughly what was about to be said, and would be able to verify much of that knowledge by means of the tape-recorder nestling in his wardrobe.

Bitter experience had taught Steve Lathan that the British, following yet another of their strange rituals, were quite capable of keeping 'business' until the coffee. As an American, he could brush all this aside and ask point-blank over the apéritifs what they were proposing to write about Isaac Erter.

Wood replied, 'We want to get at the truth. Who killed him? And why? Did the Official Inquiry ever find out? If so, why weren't we told? Or was it all fixed—a cover-up?'

Lathan grimaced. 'Quite a lot of questions! Sounds as if you don't believe the Libyans did it.'

'Do you?' asked Cameron.

'No. They'd have been publicly accused, and they weren't, so I guess the whole thing was just another load of media malarkey.'

Wood pursued the original premise. 'Official Inquiries have a habit of never talking to the right people, never asking the right questions when they do. I mean, look at the Warren Report on Kennedy's assassination!'

Lathan nodded: then smiled at his wife, who was sitting next to him, and put a hand over hers as if to draw attention to her presence. Wood smiled at her too, not only out of politeness but also, she knew, to reassure her that all the doubts and fears she had voiced at their first meeting were groundless: they had no intention of harming her husband in any way. All he said was, 'I'm afraid this is going to bore you to hell and back.'

It was on the tip of her tongue to reply, 'When I'm actually going to *learn* something about Steve!' but she merely said, 'Not at all. As a student I was an Erter fan, we all were, and I still think he had the right idea. Ignore me, I don't in the least mind being ignored.'

Wood, with his instinctive feel for man-woman relationships, knew that these two loved each other deeply, and he was more than ever pleased that Cameron had not tried to drive a wedge between them, a ploy which could only have failed, perhaps with disastrous results. Cameron himself was barely aware of the touching hands and drew no conclusion from them. He said, 'Could you tell us what happened? There was some mention of you being off duty—what did that mean? And if you were off duty, what were you doing at the Hotel Imperia?'

Lathan smiled. No waiting until the coffee here! But he paused for a long moment before answering, aware that after the moment there would be no turning back; if he was making a big mistake, this was his Rubicon.

It was ironical, but in a way perfectly just, that Cameron should misread the hesitation, saying, 'We haven't talked about what's in it for you. Our paper pays pretty well for this kind of—'

'Jesus! I don't want to be *paid*.' He spoke fiercely, but Cameron was not abashed: 'Well, that's your business. I'd take it if I were you.'

Wood caught Holly Lathan's eye and knew that they were both thinking the same thing: that never in a thousand years could David Cameron be Steve Lathan.

As if to escape from the whole contentious subject Lathan said, 'Intelligence departments are full of prima donnas, I bet you don't know that.'

This did take Cameron aback; in his experience, money was very seldom so explicitly dismissed.

'There was a fancy argument going on with the Israelis, that's why I was off duty—and as mad as hell. You couldn't understand it without knowing a bit about the procedure, and the layout.'

While they ate he described the Hotel Imperia and the separate ballroom extension which made it ideal from the security point of view. There were two means of access; it was readily agreed by all concerned that the most easily controllable plan was for the Arab delegates to use the main doors on the Piazza Aralia; the American and Jewish delegates would enter from the Via Palomina. This was not so much a side entrance as a separate entrance to a huge lobby used for various functions, exhibitions and so on. The lobby was connected with the ballroom or conference room by a wide passage. Between the lobby and the passage were massive plate-glass doors.

Tom Wood, listening with half his mind, was wondering

with the other half just how he would describe this man when the time came for writing descriptions. The blue eyes, the neat fair hair, the average good looks, belonged to the image of the standard all-American boy matured to manhood. But there was more: a kind of worn, perhaps even bewildered, sophistication. An all-American boy who had seen too much of the wicked and grubby ways of the world, and had in some way been hurt by them, perhaps by the very fact that they existed. An innocent American, violated. ('Jesus! I don't want to be *paid*!')

'Okay,' said Lathan, 'this is where the prima donnas come in, all belting out high C's.'

His wife smiled into her wine-glass; the musical jargon was about all that was left of her lengthy training; he had picked it up from her.

'The Italians were responsible for exterior security, including traffic, etcetera. We, the Americans, my own outfit, were responsible for the overall interior security of the conference hall. Also of course for the Secretary of State. That left Isaac Erter and the Israelis.'

Cameron said, 'How many Israeli delegates were there, anyway?'

'Six. But we only need worry about Erter. The original plan was that Israeli Security brought him to the hotel ten minutes after the others had arrived—they escorted him into the lobby. At the plate-glass doors, where we were on duty anyway, they handed him over to us. Easy, no problems. Then one day they suddenly announced that this didn't suit them, they wanted to bypass us and escort him right the way to the conference table. Up to that moment I'd been meeting them at the doors and taking him on from there. Now, for some reason, they didn't trust me to do that properly, me and my eight men. No sir, they wanted to do it themselves!'

He laughed, realizing that even now, after so many years, he was betraying all over again the anger he had felt at the time. Such stupid anger, talk about prima donnas!

'And that,' said Cameron, is why you were hanging about doing nothing when it happened. Off duty.'

'And mad as hell. Correct.'

They considered this in silence. Waiters descended on them in a cloud of appetizing smells and served their main courses. Wood, who was acting as host, directed operations in execrable French, and grimaced at Holly who was enjoying his efforts. He wondered why she suddenly looked happier, less confused, therefore younger and prettier.

He was not to know that she had just understood her husband's insistence that she should join them. Regarding his headaches and his nightmares, the cat had been let out of the bag at the hospital; now and here she was going to be told exactly what had caused them. This way he would be saved the embarrassing necessity of heroic revelations. Among men, Englishmen in particular, he could make a wry joke of the heroics, whereas face to face with her in the privacy of their own flat there was a danger that they might assume their true and admirable proportions. Men were extraordinary.

'Now,' said Cameron, brown eyes intense behind the lenses, 'can you tell us just what happened?'

'No, I can't.'

Both younger men bristled, sensing evasion. 'But you must have seen . . .'

'No, I didn't see a darn thing. They'd just come in at the door when this stupid jerk of an Assistant Manager grabbed me and started yakking about some party that was due to be held in the ballroom.' He looked from one disappointed face to the other. 'Yeah, that's right. I had my back to the whole shebang. First thing I knew was the shooting.'

Wood grimaced. 'He wasn't a diversion, the Assistant Manager—planned?'

'No. For a start I wasn't even supposed to be there. Also he was too dumb—it was just bad luck.'

'So you heard the shooting?'

'Correct. *Then* I turned and ran to the doors. They were locked, that was procedure. Behind them somebody was murdering Erter.'

'Did you . . .' Cameron ran a hand through his curly hair, making it stand on end. 'Did you recognize them?'

'I don't know how you react to that kind of emergency, but I'm one-track-minded, I was only thinking of one thing —how to shoot the lock off that door and get to Erter before they killed him. I don't know what I saw. I was running and shooting and grabbing the old guy and getting myself shot and then, wham! somebody gave me this wing-dinger from behind, and I was out.'

'That quick!'

'Sure. I guess I had all of . . . ninety seconds to see something. Maybe I *did* see something and the crack on the head erased it. I don't know.'

Wood said, 'So you didn't see anything—who do you *think* it was?'

'The old million-dollar-question.'

'Here's what we've been offered.' He counted on his fingers. 'Arab extremists. The American armament industry. Their contacts and middlemen. The Israelis themselves. The Red Brigade. Oh yes, the KGB.'

Cameron added, 'With the KGB as favourites, what do you think of that?'

'Nothing. When in doubt blame the Reds—too many people were pushing the idea, it doesn't feel right, who trusts a hard sell anyway?'

Cameron had caught sight of his hair in a mirror and was trying to smooth it down. 'We did three or four days' newspaper research. There was certainly no mention of the Russians at the time.'

Lathan gestured. His wife said, 'I bet you didn't research the *Weekly Mole.*'

They looked blank.

'It was a student paper. I told you we were very hot on Erter.' Cameron nodded, remembering his wife's student-like tirade on the subject. 'What did it say? Can you remember?'

'Some of it. Apparently the Official Inquiry questioned about fifty people . . .'

Lathan snorted. 'Like who? All anybody found when they got up off the floor was me, unconscious, holding Erter, dead, plus one unknown gunman, also dead, plus a second unknown gunman who died on his way to hospital.'

'What were they?' Cameron asked. 'Nationality and so on?'

'Nobody knew. Or if they did they weren't telling.'

Holly persisted: 'The *Mole* said that among those people they questioned was his bodyguard, but we never heard what came of it. That was when everybody began to think they were the ones who'd killed him.'

'Wait a minute, you've got something there!' Wood was staring at her intently; switched the green eyes to her husband. 'I didn't ask you the right question just now. This change the Israelis wanted—cutting you out, taking Erter to the conference table themselves—how long had it been going on?'

'That was the first day.'

Wood could feel Cameron's excitement jump like a spark between them. 'You mean,' he said incredulously, 'that on the very day you were taken off duty and the Israelis took over, Erter was killed?'

'Correct.'

The two journalists exchanged a look. Holly Lathan said, 'That's exactly what I meant—that's why we all thought the Israelis had done it.'

Cameron turned to her husband. 'How about that? Obviously you knew the Israeli contingent by sight.'

'Sure.'

'Did you see any of them beyond the glass doors, close to Erter?'

'That's where they should have been, so I guess that's where they were. But you know how it is when you're working with the same guys every day—they become part of the landscape, you don't really *see* them.'

'And you didn't check later?'

'As far as I was concerned, "later" was six months later, when I came out of hospital.'

'I forgot that.'

'Anyway you don't do a lot of checking in the security game, unless it's in the line of duty.'

'And in this case it wasn't.'

'In this case we were told that the Official Inquiry was taking care of the whole thing. And boy, did it ever!'

Cameron pushed his glasses up his nose. 'Perhaps there was a good reason why they didn't want you to check.'

'I don't get it.'

'I mean,' said Cameron, 'that the only potential killers we haven't considered are the Americans.'

Lathan laughed. 'We'd been given the push. My team wasn't even there. They were on the beach at Ostia or in the sack with their girlfriends. I was the only one around because I was sore, and I sure as hell didn't break down those doors, shoot Erter and myself, and then hit myself over the head with a blunt instrument.'

'Other Americans, not your team.'

'Those I *would* have recognized, I knew them all, we were all in the same unit.' He looked from one thoughtful face to the other. 'You've taken on a tough one.'

Wood nodded. 'That's what makes it good. This business about changing the security procedure, the Israelis demanded it, right?'

'Right. You've really got your teeth into them, haven't you?'

'Yes, I have. Who would have been responsible for putting that demand to the Americans?'

'Guy in charge, I guess.'

'Know his name?'
'Sure. Ben-Amir. Rafael Ben-Amir. And believe me, I'd have seen *him*—big fellow, big as you are.'
'Still around?'
'Must be. He was only . . . thirty-two, thirty-five.'
'And how did those orders come through to you?'
'From my boss. Name of Gordon McKenna.'

Wood looked at his partner. Cameron said, 'That's the next step all right. Rafael Ben-Amir and Gordon McKenna, in that order. How do we find them?'

Tennison often had no idea why he took certain actions; he had long ago grown used to the promptings of intuition or experience or whatever it was, and knew better than to ignore them. Something had suggested to him that he ought to stay in the café opposite the restaurant, and so he had stayed there, eating a passable meal and reading *France-Soir*. Nobody, as usual, took any notice of him.

Eventually instinct had drawn his attention to the street outside. It was a perfectly ordinary Parisian side-street, dominated by apartment buildings but also incorporating two cafés, a jeweller, a confiserie with a window full of enticing delicacies, three boutiques, a flower-shop and the restaurant itself. Yet something was undoubtedly wrong with it.

After three-quarters of an hour's intent watching Tennison discovered that what was wrong with it was that whereas a number of people passed by and were gone, and a certain old lady made two journeys from her apartment to the confiserie and back again, there was one figure which passed by but was not gone. This, Tennison realized, was no ordinary loiterer; the man was loitering with intent and with considerable expertise. Of course it was possible that by coincidence he was a private detective collecting the usual information about marital infidelity, but Tennison was inclined to think not. Private detectives, however diligent, usually sat in cars: partly because it was more comfortable, partly because their trade often called upon them to take clandestine photographs.

Somebody at the CIA's London station had given Lathan's address to the two journalists; the next step would be to inform the Paris station of this fact; the next step, as Anthony Markham had surmised, would be for the Paris station to put a tail either on the two Englishmen or on Lathan himself, the latter being the more likely since in the present situation Lathan was the catalyst. All in all, Tennison thought, if he was not at this very moment looking at that tail he would eat the beret which was part of his French camouflage: out of date, he knew, and thus comfortingly provincial; it also concealed the perhaps noticeable widow's peak.

He toyed with the idea of slipping out of the café and taking steps to get a good look at the man's face—it was always reassuring to be able to recognize an adversary—but on the other hand Markham had said, 'You'll have to keep a low profile, and I mean very,' adding that they were not about to take on the whole CIA. Regretfully Tennison decided that keeping a very low profile was not reconcilable with getting a closer look at the loiterer; and after all, it wasn't the man who mattered so much as the fact of his existence.

He realized with interest that the presence of this individual had induced a faint tremor of what passed, in his emotional make-up, for excitement. It was possible, just possible, that the watching man whom he was now watching might in some way constitute the weak link which Markham so badly needed him to find or to create in Paris: the all-important break in continuity.

Inside the restaurant, the problem of finding Rafael Ben-Amir and Gordon McKenna had begun to assume awkward proportions.

Once, as Lathan pointed out, he could have telephoned any of a dozen professional contacts who would have wasted no time in discovering the present whereabouts of both men; but even though he was still in touch with a few of those contacts, and occasionally sought their help regarding some problem of Industrial Peace at Lagarde et Rochet, there was no way in which he could suddenly start asking questions about the death of Isaac Erter without somebody wondering what was going on. 'Lookit, I was the only witness, I was even suspected of having killed the old guy myself.' He shook his head vigorously. 'No sir!'

His wife, who still hoped to steer the whole matter away from him, and thus from herself, said, 'You're a couple of investigative reporters, well-known, influential—surely you can ask whatever questions you like wherever you like? It's no crime to be doing a story on Isaac Erter.'

Wood sighed. 'I'm afraid that depends on various people's point of view.' And he told her about the warnings from an unknown source which each of them had received in London —including the threat that Israeli Intelligence might well deny them right of entry. They could hardly march into, say, the Israeli Embassy and announce that they wanted to talk to Rafael Ben-Amir, a *member* of Israeli Intelligence.

Lathan thought about this for a few seconds, then said, '*You* couldn't, and I couldn't, but Holly could.'

His wife instantly seized on this as a heaven-sent opportunity to get rid of the two Englishmen and all their embarrassing questions; she did not, however, allow herself to seem too eager, but was at length persuaded to undertake the mission if told exactly what to do and say.

'Easy, honey. Give a false name—pretend you're some relative, old girlfriend—you want to get in touch with Rafael after all these years. Turn on the charm, give them the bright eyes, they won't know what hit them.'

'All right. If you really think I can.' Her acquiescence ended the dinner-party on a note of hope.

As they put on their coats, Lathan said to the two younger men, 'Look, I know you're in a hurry, but believe me, in this kind of game hurry gets you no place. Take it easy, play it cool. Listen to your Uncle Steve, he's had a lot of practice.' Which made it all the more ironical that as soon as they left the restaurant, each pair going a different way, a shadow detached itself from shadow and followed Steve Lathan and his wife towards the Métro.

Tennison, following the follower, watched all three of them disappear from sight into the bowels of the earth. He had won his bet with himself and would not have to eat the beret, a negative victory perhaps but one that held possibilities. This was the link all right; could he find a weakness in it?

Seeing that Cameron and Wood were getting into a taxi, he decided to walk back to the hotel. He had always been able to think more clearly while walking.

5

David Cameron supposed that it was something to do with marriage which, in recent years, had made him so impatient. He knew that Lathan's advice had been good advice, 'hurry gets you no place, take it easy, play it cool,' but it didn't satisfy him; he wanted to get *moving*, and though he could pretend that this was because the story was an interesting one, at bottom it could only mean that he wanted to get back to his wife and children. He despised himself for such bourgeois dependence and envied his partner who now leaned back in his corner of the taxi, looking cool and easy, and thoughtful.

Cameron said, 'I liked him. Did you?'

'Very much. The nicest kind of American. David, if we go to Israel . . .'

'What do you mean "if", we've got to go—that's the matrix, hub, whatever.'

'Do you think he'd come with us?'

Cameron stared in surprise. Like many impatient people who are also intelligent, it always amazed him that slower minds ever had any really good ideas. 'Jesus!, why didn't *I* think of that?'

'Would he?'

'Yes. Behind all that self-control there's a man bursting with curiosity—my God, wouldn't *you* want to know who'd tried to kill you? We'll give him a ring as soon as we get back.'

When Tennison unlocked his wardrobe ten minutes later and took out his document-case the spools of the recorder were already turning. Direct Volume produced Wood's voice speaking on the telephone: '... and according to her, everybody thinks you ought to take a holiday in any case. Will you come? All expenses paid, naturally.'

Pause. Then, very excited: 'My God, that'd be terrific—are you sure? Yes, of course *we're* sure. We want to talk to Mrs Erter, some of the old boy's friends, that woman who ran his Peace Party ...'

From Cameron: 'Judith Kollek.'

'Judith Kollek—with people like them you'd be a ... a kind of passport, you tried to save his life.'

Another, longer pause. 'No, there's no doubt about that. Ben-Amir's vital, and we're going to find him, wherever he is. But a lot depends on what your wife can get out of the Embassy tomorrow.'

Tennison froze, staring at the machine. From it, Wood's voice said, 'By the way, is there a *Mrs* Ben-Amir? If there is, Holly had better pretend she's a relative, not an ex-girlfriend, see what I mean?'

After this Lathan talked for a full minute. Then Wood replied, 'We've discussed that, we've come to the conclusion it was just a threat. Even the Israelis think twice about barring the Press, it only gets them a lot of bad publicity—what are they trying to hide? all that sort of thing.'

Pause. 'We'd like to go as soon as possible. And, Steve, we don't *know* Ben-Amir isn't right there in Jerusalem.' Pause. 'Yes, of course, lots of things—why don't you come over here tomorrow evening. Any time. Six o'clock would be fine. Room 67. Give our regards to Holly and wish her luck.'

Sound of the receiver being replaced, and Cameron's voice: 'He's coming, I knew he would.'

'He says no problem, he'll arrange it with his boss tomorrow. Holly's going to the Embassy in her lunch-hour.'

Tennison shook his head and said to the recorder, aloud but quietly, 'No, I don't think so.'

On the other side of Paris, Steve Lathan turned to his wife and said, 'Okay, I'll take that vacation—how about Israel?' and wondered why she stared at him wide-eyed, suddenly pale.

Tennison looked at his watch. Where was Anthony Markham at this moment? He could remember without consulting his little black book: the 11th, Washington—where the time would now be . . . ten past four in the afternoon. That bright girl at the answering-service would know exactly how to contact him.

Tennison called the bright girl; then paced up and down the room, testing his conviction for strength and durability; he could find nothing wrong with it. A variable amount of time would now pass, depending on how easily Markham could get to a suitable pay-phone; nobody in Washington trusted private telephones any more, least of all a man like Anthony Markham.

Eight minutes later the night-porter called and said that a Monsieur Roberts was ringing from the United States. Monsieur Picon accepted the reversed charges. Markham's voice said, 'Yes?'

'They've talked to Lathan. They're on to Ben-Amir. They're planning to go to Israel as soon as possible—it could be the day after tomorrow.' He didn't like using the real names either of places or people, it contradicted everything he'd ever been taught. He hoped that Markham was right, as he usually was, when he said that in this case speed was infinitely more important than secrecy.

'Quick off the mark. How do they know Ben-Amir's there?'

'They don't at the moment, but they're going to find out.'

'What do you mean?'

Tennison explained what he meant in a few terse sentences, with specific allusion to the man who was tailing the Lathans; then he explained how, Markham willing, he proposed to deal with the situation and capitalize on it. 'This is the weak link you wanted. Give me the go-ahead and I'll break it.'

'Yes, I think you're right.'

'Lathan's going to Israel with them.' He heard the rhythm of Markham's breathing change, and could tell from that how surprised he was.

'You're sure?'

'He said he'd go. I don't think he's a man who'd change his mind or let anyone down.'

Silence. Tennison knew better than to interrupt it; that was how people lost their jobs. He also knew that Markham was swiftly dissecting this new eventuality, revealing its bones and fitting them into the skeleton of his plan. At length he said, 'Okay, break the link.' Tennison nodded, pleased; it was an opportunity he would have hated to miss.

'I'll send a man to Tel Aviv from London right away—fly there myself tonight. Trouble is the damn time-change. You're going to give me the hours I need, and I'm going to throw them away flying East.' Another silence. 'I want you to send a cable. At . . . yes, seven p.m. tomorrow, *Israeli* time. Message reads, "Arriving Israel tomorrow thirteen

April. Stop. Urgent repeat urgent we meet." Signed, Steve Lathan.' This was the last thing Tennison had expected, and on the face of it he could think of nothing more dangerous. He managed to say, 'Yes, I've got that.'

'Make it registered, or whatever's safest. I'll call you tomorrow night, just to check. Around . . . nine-thirty. Okay?'

'Yes.'

'Anything else?'

'No.' He waited for the click of the receiver being replaced in Washington DC; then replaced his own.

The spool of the tape-recorder had stopped turning. Tennison crouched beside it and set about replaying the beginning and end of the conversation upstairs, both of which he had missed.

In Washington, Anthony Markham walked from the Texaco station where he had made the call, around the corner, and back towards the apartment building. A warm damp wind was streaming across the Potomac which was in one of its dour moods, grey and wrinkled.

He was thinking about the old enemy, Time. Even if he flew to New York within the next hour, even if he caught El Al Flight 016 to Tel Aviv, not a direct flight unfortunately but via London, he would still be moving Eastwards to meet a day already old by the time he reached Israel. Tennison's plan would work, but could it gain him enough time to keep ahead for the vital hours, at least seven, which he must at all costs have? He realized, with irritation, that once again, but in circumstances which disallowed the slightest error, he was going to have to resort to the kind of risk he despised and never took. And all because Time was not on his side.

In that case he should have stayed in London. Impossible. New York and Santa Barbara were inessential, but nothing which had been said or was yet to be said in Washington could have been entrusted to a telephone.

He came to the pompous modern entrance, simply 'Number Thirty-Three' in stainless steel on stainless steel; pressed a button, murmured his name into a microphone, and was received into the over-heated lobby where an armed guard sat picking his teeth in front of a bank of closed-circuit television monitors. These informed him that a cat was prowling about the subterranean parking-lot and that pieces of paper were skittering along the sidewalk. Nothing else moved.

The guard, who had seen him enter this citadel two hours before, and leave it fifteen minutes ago, was now regarding him as if he represented some new kind of threat. Not wishing to be shot unquestioned, Markham said, 'Mr Atwater, remember?'

The guard nodded. He knew that Jerry Atwater was away in the Adirondacks; before going, he had left instructions to say that his apartment would be used for an important meeting on 11 April at 2.0 p.m. The guard wondered whether he was away because he didn't want to be associated with the meeting, or whether the meeting was being held in his empty apartment because the three men who were up there didn't want to be associated with Jerry Atwater. Either was possible, this was Washington, and one of the three was a Senator, a big one.

Markham knew, even before he re-entered the apartment, that the two men had been talking about him in his absence; he would have been surprised to discover that they had been talking about anything else. The Senator, whose name was Jefferson Drysdale, had been a power behind the Presidential throne for so long that even the political cartoonists, ever ready to flog dead horses, had given up portraying him in that role. The media sometimes described him as 'hawk-faced', and he liked the implied distinction, but in truth his face, the set of his balding head on skinny shoulders, were more reminiscent of a less charismatic bird, the vulture.

The other man, whom Markham had unwillingly telephoned from London, was younger, in his early forties. His name was Boyd Braunsweg. Markham had always wondered who or what it was that Boyd Braunsweg reminded him of, but oddly the answer had evaded him until now. Surely this was exactly how Nero must have looked when he was still young, reasonably sane, flabby perhaps but not yet gross? And surely the Emperor must often have worn this cold, sneering, watchful expression? Even Braunsweg's first remark was appropriately Neronic: 'I was saying you could easily have used Atwater's phone—who'd bother to bug Atwater?' The voice was smooth and soft. He smiled at his own little joke and patted his paunch.

The vulture roused itself and flapped mangy wings. Jefferson Drysdale would naturally consider himself above such petty personal comments, he who lived in a more rarefied air and breakfasted with Presidents. Dinners were two-a-penny, luncheons obligatory, but breakfasts betokened importance or intimacy or both. 'Everything going to plan?' he asked Markham.

'Nothing ever goes to plan, Senator, but it's moving, I don't ask for more.' He looked from one to the other of them. 'Could we wind up this meeting as quickly as possible? I'm going to have to catch a plane from Kennedy tonight.'

'Ah,' said Braunsweg, 'that means a foul-up.'

'If there was a foul-up I'd have said so.'

'I wonder.'

'You don't have to wonder, I've just told you.'

Nero, who had taken up position behind a large desk, thus giving the desired impression that it was he who had convened this meeting, leaned forward and fixed Markham with hard grey eyes. 'I don't like your attitude, Markham, I find it . . . insubordinate.'

'It could only be insubordinate if I was in a position of subordination, and I'm not.' He glanced at his watch. 'Forgive me, I really don't have time for childish arguments like this.'

Braunsweg hit the desk with a plump pale fist. 'Childish, eh? Let me tell you something, buddy-boy—if you succeed, don't forget I'll be the one handing out the fat jobs around here.'

'*When* I succeed, Mr Braunsweg, the last thing I'll want is a job from you, I know too much about your morals . . .'

'Morals, you son-of-a-bitch! You can't . . .'

'He means,' said Drysdale in a surprisingly resonant voice, his Congress voice, 'your political morals, Boyd, not your sexual ones. And I may say I don't think your attitude in the least suits the image which you may—or will, if Mr Markham is correct—have to project.' The vulture's eyes, when opened wide which they seldom were, had a strange and rather terrible glint to them, yellowish, almost sick. The eyes, and the scarcely veiled threat contained in his words, reduced Braunsweg to silence.

'Mr Markham,' he continued, 'is not your subordinate, neither is he mine. We, or rather you to be precise, are employing him much as you would a . . . an advertising company to promote an electoral campaign. He's a specialist, he's working for a fee.'

'A darn fat fee.'

'Which will be more than deserved if he succeeds in what we . . . you are demanding of him.' This repeated juggling of 'we' and 'you' was masterly, saying so much more clearly than words, 'If you fail in what you've hired this man to do, you'll be on your own. I personally will not be around, I'll be breakfasting with the President.'

'Okay,' said Braunsweg easily, with the kind of ease which meant that the matter had been filed and would not be forgotten, 'I seem to be outvoted on that one.' The grey eyes slid over Markham's face and then away. There was greater danger in this glance than there had been in the direct and angry stare. 'Seems to me we could have saved ourselves a lot of hassle, not to mention the fat fee, by just leaking the whole darn thing to the *Washington Post*.'

Senator Drysdale sighed. 'We've discussed this at length. More than once. Any ordinary political manœuvre, yes, we could have done that. But in this case we're dealing with the most sophisticated Intelligence force in the world. They'd be on to a leak within minutes, they wouldn't rest until they'd torn it apart and shown-up the people behind it.'

'And,' added Markham, with malice, 'a few of those would have been crucified.'

'As it is,' Drysdale continued, 'the trail is hidden every inch of the way, and the story breaks on the other side of the Atlantic. Have we got that clear? Do we need to discuss it any more—ever?'

Braunsweg knew all this perfectly well and had possibly not listened to a word. Eyes still on Markham, he said, 'I guess I'm allowed to ask my consultant, *our* consultant—' he was no fool—'just why he's leaving days earlier than planned. If it isn't a foul-up, what is it?'

'Things are moving more quickly than I anticipated.'

'Good.' The vulture nodded several times, emphatically. Nero's eyes again slid over Markham's face, and he wondered why it wasn't possible to feel them physically, why they didn't leave a mucous trail like two grey slugs. 'Excellent!' The tone was mocking, disbelieving. It prompted Markham to say, 'Before I go, there are a couple of things we'd better get straight. You told me you had a reliable informer at the London station.'

'I have.'

'Then why didn't he tell you, so you could tell me, that someone was monitoring my two journalists? Giving them Steve Lathan's address?'

'Oh, that!' Dismissively.

'That, Mr Braunsweg, is the kind of thing which screws up a whole operation.'

'If I didn't know how clever you are, Markham, I'd say you were excusing a failure in advance.'

'I told you at the start—where the CIA's concerned I

can't come out into the open and I can't stop them reporting to Washington.'

The vulture extended his scrawny neck and retracted it again. 'We have, I think, ah . . . taken care of the in-flow of information at this end. Correct, Boyd?'

'Sure. The buck stops at Clandestine Services—or if it doesn't somebody's out of a fat job.'

Markham was relieved, but didn't intend to show any such human emotion in present company. Until now he had only suspected that these two political gangsters had an ally within the fourth and largest of the CIA's Directorates. As always when working with amateurs, he made assurance doubly sure. 'No information gets past Clandestine Services, is that what you're saying?'

'Sure. How many times do I have to repeat it? You're sitting pretty.'

'No, I'm not. I have to cope with the men in the field—London, Paris, Jerusalem—and you can thank your lucky stars most of them are incorruptible.'

'Yeah, I love them too. Jesus, you're a cold fish, Markham.'

Markham considered him in silence. Jefferson Drysdale turned away to look out of the window, dissociating himself from more petty personal comments.

Markham said, 'You don't know what I am and never will—because that's the way I keep it. I'm a professional, you don't get many of those around here. Professionally, I spend ninety per cent of my time studying other people's personalities, that's the job. When it comes to yours and mine I'm not interested. All you want from me is efficiency, and that's what you'll get.'

Senator Drysdale turned. 'Which, as I recall, is why you were chosen for this undertaking.'

'Also why your man at the London Embassy ought to be fired.'

'Oh Christ!' said Braunsweg. 'Not that again!'

'Next time he may really screw you up.'

'My problem, not yours. Where are you going in such a hurry? Israel?'

'London.' He would no more have admitted to either of them that Jerusalem was his immediate destination than he would have dreamed of accepting a job in Washington DC, and he had no doubt that Braunsweg would offer him one; politicians invariably did, as invariably he declined. It was no place for a man who liked to be his own master: witness Nero, now consolidating his own position as whip-hand: 'Let's hope you finalize this thing pretty darn quick.'

Anthony Markham smiled. 'What's final in your world, Mr Braunsweg? Even Kissinger came back.' With which he left them, swiftly.

6

Holly Lathan had just finished making the bed when the telephone beside it began to ring. Her husband had left for work half an hour before; she herself had three-quarters of an hour in which to dress and be at Golden Promotions. She stared at the ringing phone; for some reason she was quite sure who was on the other end of the line. Would it be courageous not to answer it, or merely foolhardy? As much to stop the insistent din as for any other reason she reached out and lifted the receiver. The expected voice said, 'Madame Lathan?'

'Yes.'

'Thank you for carrying out my instructions.'

'Did I have any option?'

'Only unpleasant ones, I agree.'

'Yes, it *was* unpleasant, but it's done. I told my husband the whole story, so whatever it is you want now I'm not doing it. You can't . . . blackmail me any more.'

There was silence. Then the man said, 'No, no—that isn't the truth, you're not a good liar.'

'I told him everything.'

'Even if you did, Mrs Lathan, and you didn't, it would hardly alter our ... relationship. You're an intelligent woman, surely you realize by now that I'm helping you. In a somewhat brutal manner, yes, but helping all the same.'

The odd thing was that this thought had indeed slid through her mind, as slippery as an eel; she had not been able to hold on to it long enough for examination, and was taken aback to hear him voice it. He continued: 'I'll give you an example. You and your husband are being followed —by the CIA, as far as I know. You were followed from the restaurant, La Cornemuse, last night. You will be followed if you go to the Israeli Embassy in your lunch-hour, which is what you plan to do.'

She could not help catching her breath at his all-encompassing knowledge. What had she thought before? Like talking to God or one's own conscience. The omnipotence made her feel cowed, defenceless; made her little lie about telling Steve seem absurd.

'When the man who's following you hears that you're trying to discover the present whereabouts of Rafael Ben-Amir ...'

She must have let out some helpless sound, because he said, 'Sit down, Mrs Lathan, I know this must seem very frightening. If you could convince yourself that I'm on your side it will be easier to take.'

Obediently she sat on the bed. Defiance was so obviously useless.

'As soon as he hears you ask that question you'll be in danger—but nothing compared to the danger which will face your husband.' He let this sink in; then added, 'Does what I've said about the CIA make sense to you, or shall I explain it further?'

'They don't . . . don't want Steve to give any more information about the death of Isaac Erter.'

'That's roughly correct. Now here's what I want you to do. You must *on no account* go anywhere near the Embassy, but you'll tell your husband you've been there.' He heard her intake of breath. 'Yes, more lies, I'm afraid, but these will be the last. You must tell him they were most helpful. It didn't take them more than half an hour and one telephone call to Jerusalem, for which you paid, to find out that Mr Ben-Amir has retired from Intelligence and is now living in Israel. He has become an irrigation engineer. Do you understand.'

'Yes.'

'That's what you tell your husband.'

'Yes, but the idea of my going . . .'

'Rafael Ben-Amir's present address is as follows—have you got a pencil?'

'Yes.'

'Number 19, Abba Hayil.' He spelled it slowly, allowing for the effect of shock upon her thought-processes. 'Have you got that?'

'Number 19, Abba Hayil.'

'Naturally you asked where it is. They showed you a map. It's in the Jordan Valley, about sixty miles north of the Dead Sea, four hundred feet below sea-level. Have you got that?'

'Yes.'

'It might be a good idea to tell your husband you thought you were being followed. He may already know—if not, he'll be warned. You're very silent.'

'I suppose . . .'

'What?'

'It's no good asking who you are, why you're . . . so interested in this business.'

'None at all. And I needn't add that if you fail to do as I ask . . .'

'Please. I know that.'

'Kindly repeat to me exactly what you're going to do.'

She repeated the whole rigmarole, reading the address, even noting how far Abba Hayil was below sea-level. As she did so, she was aware of a most unexpected emotion stealing over her. At any moment he was going to ring off, leaving her alone with all this secret knowledge; she was amazed to realize that she didn't want him to ring off, that his presence gave her an odd feeling of security.

'Very good. If you do as I say and keep this information strictly to yourselves you'll be in no immediate danger.'

'All right. I . . .'

'Yes?'

'Nothing.'

'Goodbye, Mrs Lathan. I don't think I'll be troubling you any more.' On the previous occasion, it was true, he had said, 'Au revoir.'

She echoed him. 'Goodbye.'

Tennison returned from the café's telephone-box to a table where a pot of coffee and two croissants were waiting for him. While he ate his breakfast he considered what he had done and what effect it would probably have.

Certainly a link had been broken; nobody could now know that they were in possession of Rafael Ben-Amir's address, which meant that nobody knew they were intending to contact him; therefore nobody could possibly know that they planned to go to Israel immediately. Even this simple lack of information would gain valuable time; had already gained it.

Much would now depend on how and when they left Paris. Tennison was reasonably sure that since Lathan had decided to accompany the newspapermen he would take steps to cover his movements and, with any luck, theirs; he was a trained security officer and aware of the fact that he was courting danger, even if he didn't realize how great that danger was; he would be doubly alerted when his wife mentioned that she thought she was being followed. Any evasive action he then took could only widen the rift in time which Tennison had created.

Meanwhile Markham was long ago airborne from New York and consequently ahead of his adversaries. Whether he could maintain this lead in view of the time he must lose because of the eastward flight was the open question: a delicate predicament teetering on the point of imbalance.

On this day, 12th April, when Anthony Markham arrived in Israel and at once began to move very swiftly indeed, the situation in Paris came to a standstill, giving rise to a nerve-racking day.

Cameron wrote a rambling letter to his wife, and then pursued culture at the Jeu de Paume and the Grand Palais, but his mind was not really on other people's creativity. Wood roughed out a possible framework for their story, tore it up, and lunched alone and grandly. He played eye-games with an attractive woman; despite her escort, he knew that he could quite easily arrange to spend the afternoon in bed with her; it said a great deal about his state of mind that he didn't even want to. He then made up for this unusual lack of sexual dash by taking a walk in the Bois. The wind had dropped, but the afternoon was dead and dank, feeling more like autumn than spring.

Holly Lathan spent her lunch-hour buying an evening meal. She carried out one or two childish manœuvres in an effort to discover if she was really being followed, saw nobody, and wondered whether the man on the telephone hadn't been lying after all. In fact, the man on the telephone was a little way behind her, following the man who was following Holly Lathan. This period of waiting had shaken even Tennison's equilibrium; by way of a cure he had persuaded himself that he ought to ensure that she didn't after all go to the Israeli Embassy; also that he ought to take a closer look at her shadow. He knew that neither precaution was in the least necessary and he would have done better to sit quietly in the hotel and finish the current detective story, a good one.

All in all, it was a relief for all of them when Steve Lathan got home a little before six. His wife, feeling like Judas, kissed him and gave him the necessary information wrapped up in the necessary lies: Rafael Ben-Amir, 19 Abba Hayil, in the Jordan Valley some sixty miles north of the Dead Sea.

Lathan, who was in a high good humour, told her she was a clever girl and had better start packing; he had arranged with Lagarde et Rochet to be away for a week. All she had been able to think about since he first mentioned the idea of going to Israel was an imaginary meeting, a lot less unlikely than she assumed, at which Judith Kollek said to him, 'Oh, so you married that nice little girl after all,' thereby spilling the whole mess of beans. She didn't in the least want to go to Israel, but the thought of Steve going without her was unthinkable. Dutifully she considered garments for a hot climate, while he went over to the Hotel de la Tour.

Wood and Cameron, not to mention Tennison once again on Direct Volume, were relieved to hear that everything had been settled with Lagarde et Rochet, and they quickly saw the sense of his taking his wife with him. After all, as he pointed out, he was supposed to be going on vacation and would hardly leave her behind. There was also a more sinister consideration; she had an idea she was being followed; whether this was true or not (and Lathan had taken precautions when coming to the hotel), she would present a sitting target if left alone in Paris. Her husband had no intention of putting her in any such position, nor of putting himself and the two Englishmen in a position where her safety could be used against them.

This professional attention to detail made complete sense

to Tom Wood, but he could almost see his partner's well-known impatience coming to the boil. Cameron said, 'Okay, fine! There's an El Al flight at two o'clock tomorrow, how about that?'

Lathan gave him a sardonic look, accepted a Scotch, and sat down with it, considering them both analytically, blue eyes astringent. He said, 'Look—so you played pat-ball with the Mafia on your Vatican story and you got on the wrong side of the Commies over trade unions . . . but Isaac Erter's something different and I'm not too sure you dig that.'

Tennison, lying on his bed, nodded agreement.

'If your story turns out the way we all think it might you're going to end up accusing a *government* of murder, and that ain't peanuts. Also, whatever happened, don't forget that powerful guys in several countries went to a hell of a lot of trouble to stage a cover up. Reputations are going to hit the dust and some of them will stay there.'

'Certainly,' said Cameron, 'but we're only journalists.'

'And I'm only an ex-security officer, but we'd all look the same dead.'

'So?' asked Wood, who had been keeping quiet.

'So we play this my way, we take precautions. You don't fool any Intelligence outfit for long, but even if you only fool them for twenty-four hours that's a lot of time.'

Wood, aware of Cameron's impatience, said quickly, 'What are you suggesting?'

'It's not a suggestion, it's a condition of my coming in on the act. If you think I'm being over-cautious, say so, I won't be offended. Holly and I can go to . . . Madrid, she'd like that.'

Cameron managed to control himself and reply, 'No. We want you with us—that's the angle, that's the difference.'

'Okay. Here's how it goes. First thing tomorrow, you two fly back to London. Nice and easy, mission accomplished. Wouldn't be a bad idea to call your editor, as publicly as possible, tell him you got a nice interview with me and you're coming home.'

'Is that necessary?' Wood asked. 'I don't think we're being watched.'

'I wouldn't bet on it. If *we* are, why not you? At Heathrow you disappear—Gents, VIP lounge, wherever. Then you do a quick about-turn and catch El Al Flight 016, departing 9.40. Okay?'

'You're the boss.' Cameron's tone barely concealed his intolerance of all this mumbo-jumbo.

'Holly and I are going to Venice—via Milan where we suddenly change our minds. The four of us meet up in Jerusalem tomorrow afternoon. You get in at 4.15, we'll already be there. Where were you planning to stay?'

'No idea,' said Wood. 'The King David?'

'Make it the Seven Gates—it's owned by an Arab syndicate, they don't encourage bugging and other games. Okay?'

'Okay.'

'I'll book you in under a phoney name, you can always give them the real ones on arrival. And I'll get your tickets—when it comes to this kind of thing I *do* know all the right people.' He laughed. 'If you could see your faces!'

Wood said, 'Looks as if we're going to find out a thing or two about security before we've finished.'

'Before we've finished,' Lathan replied, 'we're going to find out who killed Isaac Erter.' A resolution with which not even Cameron could find fault.

Two floors below them, Tennison was feeling moderately pleased with himself: he had assessed Lathan's character correctly.

Anthony Markham had said that he would telephone at 9.30, but it was closer to 11.0 when the call from Jerusalem finally came through. Tennison wasn't paid to ask questions, and in any case Markham's voice told him a great deal of the story; he had never heard it so eroded by fatigue, though it betrayed no erosion of confidence. However much time the eastward flight had lost him, he had evidently made good use of what was left of the 12th of April. However, time still pursued him relentlessly, and he was delighted to hear that Lathan had procured a little more of it for him by bullying Cameron and Wood into concealing their true destination. 'Where are they going to stay?'

'The Seven Gates.'

'Good. I'll move over there right now. Accommodation isn't a problem, by the way—no tourists, too much terrorism. You sent that cable.'

'Seven p.m. Israeli time. It would have got to Abba Hayil hours ago.'

'I'll check. It's important, I've already staked a life on it. As soon as they've all left Paris I want you to fly straight here. What name?'

'Victor Picon. French citizen.'

'Somebody will meet you at Lod. And they'll be holding a room at The Seven Gates. Call me as soon as you've checked in—Roberts.'

And so Steve Lathan and Rafael Ben-Amir began to move inexorably towards one another: the irony being that neither of them knew (as did Anthony Markham and others) that they were like two high-tension cables, perfectly harmless if kept apart but capable, when brought together, of creating a formidable explosion. And a concomitant power-failure in high places.

Part Three

JERUSALEM

'If you go about asking loaded questions you must expect a few loaded answers.'

1

At five o'clock on the afternoon of 12th April, when the four people in Paris were waiting for Steve Lathan to settle his affairs at Lagarde et Rochet, Anthony Markham was being driven towards Jerusalem through pine forests and across stony valleys, olive and eucalyptus punctuated by straight dark cypresses; it was a harsh landscape, but comparatively fertile and pleasant by the standards of Israel, facing the Mediterranean and its rain. Cicadas kept up their ceaseless whizz and whirr.

Paul Benedict, who had made such a telling appearance in Cameron's London garage, was at the wheel. He had been in Israel for the best part of twenty-four hours, asking questions and making arrangements; one of the latter was the battered-looking but in reality brand new Range-Rover in which they were riding; another was the gun which he now produced from under his seat and handed to Markham. He unwrapped it from its oily cloth and slipped it into his pocket. 'Still know all the right people, don't you?'

Benedict regaled him with an up-to-date account of the thriving underworld of Tel Aviv, an aspect of the Promised Land which affronted many visitors. Markham smiled at the description, but grimly, his thoughts elsewhere. Benedict could sense the tension and urgency which gripped him, and because of it knew that the business in hand, whatever that business might be, was approaching some kind of climax.

At Lod Airport he had been looking for the usual immaculate Markham, wearing a lighter suit in view of the heat but otherwise sartorially faultless; he was slow to recognize the hefty man, wearing a day's growth of stubble and sand-coloured denim, a canvas bag slung over one shoulder, no other luggage. It had suddenly struck him that the reason why Markham presented to the world such an elegant and impeccable façade, was that as soon as he allowed it to slip he looked what he really was: a tough and ruthless mercenary.

In spite of the tension, or perhaps to alleviate it a little, he asked, 'Where are we going, guv?'

'Abba Hayil. About sixty miles north of the Dead Sea.'

Benedict grimaced. 'Good thing you didn't arrive at midday.'

'I wish to hell I had.' His tone only emphasized the urgency. All the same he knew what Benedict meant. After the damp of Washington and the airless womb of the Boeing, this glaring heat, even so late in the day, was an ordeal as well as a pleasure; at noon, and in the Valley of the Jordan, it would merely have been an ordeal. He glanced at the younger man, amused by the fact that in his cast-off army clothes the dedicated Londoner looked like any other young and bearded Israeli: minus the kapel, but then many of the young men never wore it except on the Sabbath, if then. 'How's the holy land?'

'Bloody awful as usual. Bomb in some cinema last night, no hot water in the hotel this morning—that's what they call Jewish cause and effect, there's a Hebrew word for it.'

'Not very charitable, are you?'

'I like Jews—some of my best friends!—it's Israel I don't like. We've always been vagrants, we don't know how to make a home in this place—Solomon's dead, so's David.' He changed down, cursing, and passed a lumbering Army vehicle. 'As soon as we get a country, what do we do? Start fighting, making life hard for ourselves. If life isn't hard we don't like it. Me, I go to a nice synagogue in London, that's where I belong.'

Over Jerusalem there hung a strange dusty haze, apocalyptic; it made the ancient towers seem more fabled than ever, and threw a decent veil across the modern architectural monstrosities which lie to the west, ruining every westward view. The Dome of the Rock, crowning beauty of the Old City, shone dimly like a great golden pearl.

They had been silent for a long time. Benedict tried, 'What's at this place anyway?'

'Research station—geology, agriculture . . .'

'Blimey! What do they think they're going to grow—stones?'

It was comparatively cool on the bare highlands beyond Jerusalem. In this vast emptiness a group of black tents drew the eye and focused it: the timeless inhabitants of the timeless land, ignoring frontiers, moving with the seasons as their forefathers had moved for thousands of years.

Then they dropped over the ridge and into the terrible mountainous desert of Judaea. A dead weight of heat enfolded them, intensifying as they descended towards the Jordan: lower, out of the sunlight which still belaboured the dusty shimmering hills on the Arab side: lower, and hotter, and the river itself came into view, a dead grey snake leading to a dead sea through a wilderness of cracked mud rimed with salt. Godforsaken desolation. At the sight of it Benedict groaned into his beard.

Markham said, 'It'll be getting dark when we arrive. That means no chance of casing the place. I lost a lot of time on that flight, best part of a day, I'm not sure where I stand.' Benedict chose not to question this, but Markham presumably decided that it required elaboration anyway. 'Where I stand as regards The Company. We've got to get in, talk to a man, get out again quickly. If they're there before us . . .' He didn't need to elaborate this one; Benedict had first-hand knowledge of the CIA, as well as of Israeli Intelligence.

'We'll have to trust to luck and play it by ear.'

'Suits me.'

'And no shooting! That gun's only for scaring people.' He knew that Benedict loved guns, loved firing them. His collection of firearms, ancient and modern, was said to be remarkable.

They had reached the floor of the valley and were now heading north. Light was fading rapidly in the lee of the harsh mountains. Peering ahead, Markham said, 'I'm told it's just a few prefabricated huts along a track on the left of the road. We want Number Nineteen. I've no idea what kind of reception we'll get, you'd better stick your big foot in the door—and talk Hebrew.'

'Pleasure.' A dark, almost mocking glance. 'Am I allowed to ask who he is?'

'Rafael Ben-Amir, ex Israeli Intelligence.'

'Why ex?'

'Good question.'

Abba Hayil was no more and no less than he had said: a few prefabricated huts on either side of a dusty track, lost in the wasteland. Not a breath of air, only the dead encompassing heat and the dead encompassing desolation. At the end of the track, where a church might have stood in a Western settlement, was the pumping-station, temple to the god of the desert. If the researchers had managed to coax anything green out of the dust it didn't show in the fading light. No. 19 was the last hut on the right-hand side, facing No. 20. Two women chatting outside No. 7 watched the Range-Rover intently as it passed. When it came to a standstill, staring faces appeared at the window of No. 18.

Markham said, 'Stay close, cover me. But keep an eye on this vehicle. If we have to move we'll be in a hurry. Right?'

'Right.'

'Here we go!' They both got out of the Range-Rover at the same instant and converged on the door of No. 19, which was ajar. Israeli pop music, insignificant and forlorn in this forbidding place, issued from within.

Benedict inserted a large boot into the gap and called out cheerily in Hebrew, 'Hello there, anyone home?'

The door was opened by a sturdy young woman in her middle twenties: fair hair, black eyes, peasant good looks, more wonder than welcome in her regard. 'Shalom.'

'Shalom. We're looking for Rafael Ben-Amir.'

'He'll be back in a minute, he just popped over the road.'

In English, Markham said, 'May we come in?'

She stood aside. 'Is across with mining.' Her accent was Jewish-Polish; she came of a long tradition of hospitality, but was not sure of these two strangers. Markham thought it possible that she had never been sure of anything in her whole life.

Benedict, by the door, said, 'He's coming now. My God, he's a giant!'

The girl laughed. 'Very big man, Rafael.'

Entering, filling the doorway, he towered over Anthony Markham who was no dwarf. He had sharp black eyes, the whites seeming brilliant against skin burned to mahogany by sun and wind. His hair was jet-black, no trace of grey in it, nor in the truculent black moustache, though he was certainly in his forties. There was also moderation in his deep voice, betraying the fact that, like many big men, he was fundamentally a gentle one. 'What can I do for you?'

'I need to talk to you. My name's Roberts, Andrew Roberts. This is Paul Benedict.'

The black eyes examined the strangers carefully. 'What do you want to talk about?'

'Old friend of yours, Steve Lathan. Used to be in the CIA —Intelligence Security.'

Ben-Amir nodded. Impossible to say what the name meant to him or whether he was surprised to hear it; he had been trained to conceal such reactions. But he nodded; said to the girl, 'Ruth, why not some beer?' and waved towards a table around which stood four chairs. The furnishings of the hut were stark, government issue; it was as if nobody had dared to add a personal touch for fear it might take root, transforming Abba Hayil into home; that would have been a contradiction in terms, even in Israel.

They sat down facing each other. The girl, Ruth, turned off the radio, put a can of beer and a glass in front of each man. Benedict drank his by the door, one eye on the Range-Rover.

Ben-Amir said, 'Lathan was never a friend of mine, only a . . . a business associate.'

'Yes, I know that.' Markham leaned forward. 'Have the CIA been here—or your own Intelligence? Are they here now?'

'No. Why should they be?'

'Because Steve Lathan is on his way to Israel to see you.'

This was a shock, and the dark face even betrayed it.

'You know what that means, and so do I.'

'I think,' said the big man in his deep and moderate voice, 'that I'd better ask you to go.'

Markham ignored him. 'Lathan will come here to Abba Hayil—with two journalists. They're investigating the death of Isaac Erter.'

No answer. The black eyes very intent.

'When you left Intelligence you were ordered not to discuss this death with anybody.'

'Then I'll refuse to discuss it with *them*.'

'You think that'll make any difference?' He shook his head. 'The very fact that Lathan and these two men are coming to see you is enough—why do you think I asked whether the CIA or your own people were already here? They can't take the risk, they'll kill you anyway.'

The girl came forward hesitantly, biting a finger in agitation. The man reached out to touch her and calm her.

'For God's sake,' said Markham, 'admit it. Or are you just going to sit here and die?'

Suddenly the girl burst out in Hebrew, a flood of anguish. Markham turned swiftly to Benedict. Benedict said, 'She's telling him he knows you're right, he has often said the same thing himself.'

'She's got more sense than he has.'

'All right then.' Ben-Amir threw up both hands. 'I admit it. I've lived with this danger ever since Erter's death.'

'*And for no reason!*'

At this the other man's head jerked up. Their eyes met and held fast. Markham continued: 'The danger only exists as long as you say nothing, don't you see that? You're threatening your own life with your own silence. Once you've spoken out, publicly, you're safe. From their point of view there's no more harm you can do.'

The girl said, 'Is true, is true!'

Ben-Amir silenced her angrily in Hebrew; then relented and put an arm around her waist, drawing her to him. Softly, he said. 'Yes, it *is* true. And I have no wish to sit here and die.'

'Right. I came to make a deal with you, and we have very little time. Please listen carefully because I've given it a lot of thought and it makes sense. You're only in danger *before* you meet Lathan.'

The Israeli nodded, stroking his fierce moustache.

'If Lathan comes here you won't be alive to speak to him, we're agreed on that. Therefore I ask you to come with me and meet him in secret. This is the only way you can save your life. Once the meeting's over, *and they know about it*, you're in the clear.'

'But there's more, much more. If I disappear . . .'

'If you disappear, and the CIA or your old friends from Intelligence come looking for you, and they will, the first thing they'll ask is, "Where is he?" Your wife . . .'

'We're not married. Ruth.'

'Ruth will say, "He went away because he knew this man Lathan was coming. He knows Lathan is dangerous, he has too much sense to stay and meet him," all the things you said to me just now.'

'But how could I know . . . ?'

'A telegram will arrive this evening, from Paris where Lathan lives, telling you he's coming to Israel tomorrow, wants to talk to you. Ruth will show them the telegram and say, "This is what made Rafael decide to go." And she can elaborate any way you think best.'

Silence. In one of the other huts a woman was laughing, wonderful uninhibited, side-cracking laughter; humankind, that odd unknown quantity, was forcing back the wilderness, telling it to bide its time. Rafael Ben-Amir reached for his beer, finished it, wiped the moustache with the back of his hand. 'I have a brother in Haifa. Also there has been a muddle over pumping equipment—I need to go to the port at Ashdod, everyone here knows that.'

'You mean you'll come with me? Now?'

Ben-Amir considered this for what seemed to Markham, and to the girl, judging by her expression, an eternity. Benedict, at the door, shouted in Hebrew, 'Don't you touch that—go on, get out!' And to the room, 'Kids.'

'I think,' said Markham to the man opposite him, 'that it's the only way you stay alive.'

'What do you gain from this?'

'I want you to tell these men what you know about Isaac Erter's death.'

'Why?'

'I can't tell you. That's my side of the deal—that and the understanding that I'm never mentioned. Not much to ask in exchange for your life!'

Ben-Amir put down his glass and stood up, towering. 'All right, I'll come with you. I have little choice.'

'None at all, I'd say.' Markham also stood up. Benedict, who knew him well, could sense the violence of his relief, nobody else would have suspected it; nor the fact that it had robbed him of all energy and that he was suddenly almost too weary to stand.

Ben-Amir took the girl by the shoulders and turned her

to face him. 'This won't be easy for you. You're going to have to lie, and lie beautifully. You're not good at that.'

She nodded, trusting gaze fixed on his face. 'For you, very good lie.' Markham realized that he had been wrong; whatever life had taught her, she was at least sure of this one man. Ben-Amir glanced back at him. 'You talk as if I was in possession of great secrets. I'm not. I told the Official Inquiry all I knew about Isaac Erter's death, and it was nothing. I know nothing.'

Markham said, 'Put it another way—you don't know what you know.'

At a little before eleven o'clock that same night—in fact as soon as he got back to Jerusalem—Markham called Tennison in Paris, sounding as weary as he felt. As a result of their conversation Rafael Ben-Amir was quietly and quickly installed in a suite on the top floor of the Hotel of the Seven Gates: under a false name, needless to say. For his own safety, a euphemism which both men fully understood, Markham arranged for Paul Benedict to sleep on a sofa in the sitting-room.

In this same conversation Tennison also reported that on the following morning Wood and Cameron would start their journey to Israel, via London, and the Lathans via Milan. One particular part of the pattern was therefore complete. Markham knew that somehow or other, in spite of the tricks time had played on him, he had managed to stretch this crucial 12th of April to its utmost limit, thereby outwitting the old enemy. He fell into bed and slept.

2

Tennison was the first to arrive, at 11.00 a.m. He was met at Lod Airport by a taciturn Arab who drove him to the Seven Gates without speaking a word. As soon as he had registered, Tennison called Mr Andrew Roberts. Markham told him to stand by, not to leave the hotel; it would presently be necessary for him to change rooms.

The Lathans arrived at three in the afternoon, and the two journalists an hour and a half later. During their flight from London David Cameron had referred more than once to the man who had trapped him in his garage and warned him so explicitly about the ruthlessness of Israeli Intelligence. By the time they disembarked at Lod he was in a state of extreme anxiety in spite of all his partner's soothing reassurances. In fact Tom Wood had found reassurance increasingly difficult to sustain, because the tension was catching and he himself now expected to be told to get on the next plane back to London.

The high point of this ordeal came when they handed their passports to the Immigration Officer who immediately consulted an alphabetical list on his desk. When he looked up at them it was to reveal a steely and searching glare which confirmed their worst fears. However, this scrutiny turned out to be no more than a habit intended to impress; he returned the passports and wished them a happy stay in Israel.

Thus it was partly pure relief that made them greet Steve Lathan and his wife with such ebullience. To her they were like three small boys released from school and ready for adventure; she was quite unable to share their enthusiasm, partly because she had no taste for dangerous male games, partly because she was unable to comprehend very much beyond her own personal dilemma. She seemed to be in a state of suspended animation. The flight, Israel under its brilliant sun, Jerusalem which she had always wanted to visit, the sprawling luxury of their suite—all were unreal to her. Only one thing was real.

So that when she heard Cameron actually speak the name, Kollek, she felt that she must have screamed out loud, but of course she had made no sound. Luckily she was not in the room with them, but sitting on the bed doing her nails. She remained perfectly still, brush poised, and heard Tom Wood reply, 'Yes, Judith Kollek and then Mrs Erter. We've got to find out where they live.'

Her husband said, 'But Ben-Amir first.'

'Of course. Will he be on the phone?'

'I doubt it, not personally. I'd guess they only have one in those experimental places, probably in the office—we can leave it to the hotel switchboard.'

'Now?'

'Why not? While we're calling the odds. At least, I think we're calling the odds, time will tell.' At which point his wife appeared in the bedroom door and said, 'I'm going to get my hair done. I can't stand this bird's nest any longer.' There had been no time before leaving Paris and she had bewailed the fact more than once; none of the three men showed any surprise: women were always worrying about their hair even when, as now, it looked charming.

She escaped from the room; went down to the lobby; enlisted the aid of one of the porters, young and susceptible, to help her with the foreign directory. He found what she wanted very quickly. Judith Kollek still lived in Jerusalem. Ten minutes by taxi, he assured her, the city was small.

The voice which answered the telephone sounded weary and listless, not the voice she remembered; but then her heart was pounding so loudly in her ears that she could hear nothing properly. 'Olivia Osborne? Yes, yes—London, of course.'

'I . . . I need to talk to you. Now. It's . . . important.' What a word to describe the agony, the years of painful indecision and gnawing guilt. Important! Presumably the urgency inside her permeated the flat words. If she wished, said Judith Kollek, she could come round right away.

The adoring young porter summoned a taxi.

Judith Kollek lived in a small flat which had been furnished twenty-five years before and barely touched since that time: a period piece, Israeli Utility: the abode of a busy woman too absorbed in ideas and ideals to care where it was that she laid her head or made a piece of toast for her breakfast. She had once been married, but her husband had long ago grown weary of tending a political machine, let alone sleeping with one. Besides, she had always been in love with Isaac Erter, as nuns are in love with Christ.

Holly Lathan was shocked at the sight of her. Was this the dynamic, indomitable campaigner she had known in London, this shapeless woman with untidy grey hair, a heavy walk, blank eyes, bearing some indefinable and indefinably Jewish aura of suffering? But she had not lost the old acuity, and noticed the younger woman's reaction before she could hide it.

'Yes, yes, I've changed, I don't need you or anyone else to tell me.'

'I'm sorry.'

'Why? You were always a truthful child and you still are.'

'Oh no—no, I'm not! That's why I had to see you . . .' And then it was easy to let it all pour out, the whole agonized story of her stupid deception.

But as she told it, a strange metamorphosis began to occur. First of all the agony seemed to wither, overwhelmed by the stupidity; then, since stupidity is always a trivial thing . . . Yes, as she spoke she could see it all turning into something purely absurd, a kind of comic-opera libretto, under the scrutiny of this powerful woman who had in her own lifetime experienced heaven knew what pains and persecutions.

'Child, child! You should have told him, but you know that. You *must* tell him.'

'If only I could!'

'You will—here in Israel. My country has many faults, oh God, many, many faults, but there's a terrible truth in it. Not surprising when a whole people is created out of misfortune. Look at what it did to me.'

'I don't understand.'

'Nonsense! Your eyes have already understood, I saw them. A dead woman, uh? Forgotten.'

'But people . . . Thousands of people all over the world remember you—and Isaac Erter.'

'Ach, memories! I detest memories.' The eyes were no longer blank, but so full of misery that they made Holly ashamed of herself, of her own infantile woe. The flat voice said, 'Do you know what they did to me? They stoned me. In my own street my neighbours stoned me. At the hospital they thought I was dead.'

'But . . . why?'

'Peace is a filthy word to a lot of people, a sacrilege. All my life I fought for peace, I believed it was the most beautiful idea in the world, and they stoned me—smeared me with donkey's dung and called me a traitor and left me for dead.'

The younger woman, stricken by shock, heard the telephone ring but as if it was in another world. 'No, I'm sorry, not now. I'm going out. At . . . seven o'clock this evening. Good, I'll expect you then.' Only when she replaced the receiver and said, 'That was your husband,' did stupid Olivia Osborne slowly return from the dusty, sun-blasted street and the howling crowd, the cruel stones and donkey's dung: return to this small, unhappy, stifling room.

'Isaac used to say, "It's all a matter of moment. At the right moment you can create a miracle, at the wrong moment you can only create havoc." There had been an incident, they had blown up a bus and killed seventeen children—and I was talking about peace!' A shrug with both hands spread, a gesture as old as her race. 'Now I have learned to keep my mouth shut. But you . . . you must learn to open yours and tell the truth. That's why I told you those things, to shock you.'

'Yes, I was . . . am shocked.'

'For five years you have lived with a lie. For twenty-five I lived with a lie, believing that mankind wants peace. Idiot!

Mankind wants no such thing or he would long ago have attained it. Mankind wants violence and war and destruction, it's built into us and it will destroy us. Peace was my lie, that's what they made me face out there in the street.' From something like an inverted reflection of the old fire, her face returned to apathy. She put out a cool wrinkled hand and touched the young woman's smooth warm one; it was like being touched by a lizard. 'I am cured now, but it was my whole life so I am also nothing. The sooner we face our lies, the less they can hurt us. Of course, I'll keep your secret, but *you* must lose it. Quickly.'

Ruth, brought to the single telephone at Abba Hayil, told her story with muddled conviction, helped not a little by the Polish-Jewish accent and her rudimentary knowledge of the English language: 'Rafael no here. To Ashdod for pumping. Pumping from Italy not arrive since three weeks. He is Ashdod. No, I am not known where. He telephone at eight tonight. About pumping. I speak and give your telephone. Give me your telephone. No, more slower, I write it.'

'God knows,' said Wood, replacing the receiver, 'whether anything will come of that.'

Lathan smiled. 'Israel. But it'll work, it always does somehow or other.'

His wife returned from seeing Judith Kollek a few minutes before the three men left to see Judith Kollek. She said that the hotel hairdresser had been fully booked, that she had found a place in the town—which was the truth.

When they had gone she lay down on the bed and thought about peace and about the savagery which enabled ordinary people to hurl stones at a woman until they had all but killed her. 'The sooner we face our lies, the less they can hurt us.' So easy to say—but how? She rolled off the bed and began to pace to and fro. 'It's all a matter of moment —at the right moment you can create a miracle.' But would the right moment ever come?

The man who could answer that question, and would do so within a few hours, was also pacing to and fro in a suite three floors above her head. Rafael Ben-Amir knew that the waiting was necessary, but knowlege didn't make it any easier to bear. He wondered whether the CIA or his ex-colleagues of Israeli Intelligence had yet been to Abba Hayil (they had) and whether faithful Ruth had told her lies convincingly (he would have been proud of her performance, so stumbling and awkward that it positively shone with veracity).

Paul Benedict, still in residence for Ben-Amir's 'safety', pointed to the small chessboard which accompanied him everywhere and said, 'Come on, let's have another game.'

Anthony Markham, waking as a new man from that badly needed sleep, immediately began to supervise whatever makeshift arrangements were possible in the time at his disposal.

He already knew the general gist of the conversation which would presently take place between Steve Lathan and Rafael Ben-Amir, but it was essential for him to be kept informed about the results of that conversation. To this end Tennison was now installed next to the sitting-room of the suite occupied by David Cameron and Tom Wood. This was where the meeting would be held and where any ensuing decisions would be made.

Had Tennison been able to bring his voice-activated tape-recorder into Israel there would have been no difficulties, but the zeal of Israeli Customs and Security precluded any such measure, and the machine had been left with Monsieur Lamartine, the key-maker, near the Gare St Lazare. Tennison was at this moment out in the streets purchasing bits and pieces with which to manufacture a substitute.

In Markham's cast of puppets, the two journalists were now being moved towards the centre of a stage hitherto dominated by Steve Lathan. It was all going to plan, yet small doubts kept nibbling at the edges of the puppet-master's mind. Instinct told him that all was not well with the production, and he couldn't for the life of him see where the fault lay.

He reviewed his cast with care. Lathan, his wife, Ben-Amir, Wood, Cameron: all seemed to be in their correct positions and speaking their correct lines. A very minor flaw lay in the fact that Tom Wood, alone among his travelling companions, had met Markham face to face and would be extremely suspicious were he to catch a glimpse of him here and now in Jerusalem; but Markham was registered as Andrew Roberts and did not propose to leave his room for more than a few minutes until the play was over.

As for the joint efforts of Israeli Intelligence and the Jerusalem station of the CIA, they probably knew, from the telegram, that Steve Lathan had arrived in Israel, and they might well check all the hotels to find out where he was staying. No harm in that. They also knew, from the same source, that he had come to see Rafael Ben-Amir, but they had been told that Ben-Amir was avoiding him and, since Lathan posed a threat to his life, would find the notion eminently believable.

If they were really nervous they would probably search Ashdod and Haifa, where Ben-Amir's brother lived, in order to find him and warn him, or even to kill him; it would prove a long and frustrating search. They might even stake out the Hotel of the Seven Gates in case Ben-Amir lost his reason and decided, after all, to go there and talk to Lathan. But they would certainly never think of looking for Ben-Amir *in* the hotel itself where he had already been hiding behind a false name for some twenty hours. It was the hours that counted, those vital hours of the preceding day which Markham and Tennison between them had fought so hard to gain, and about which the CIA and Israeli Intelligence knew nothing whatever.

Yet despite all this self-reassurance the puppet-master remained uneasy. It had happened before, and there had always turned out to be a good reason for it. But why now? Was there a defect? If so, where? He began to re-examine the whole interlocking design all over again.

Meanwhile Tennison was enjoying himself. By a lengthy process of trial and error, and with his ear to a tumbler pressed against the wall (a child's trick but a useful one) he had found an acoustical weak point near the floor on the far side of his bed. This he had marked with a faint pencilled cross.

His purchases consisted of a small cassette-recorder, a roll of adhesive tape, a rubber teat for a baby's bottle, and two stethoscopes as used by doctors. He now bound the earpieces of one of the stethoscopes tightly against the recorder's tiny microphone and covered the whole with the rubber teat; then he held the stethoscope against the pencilled mark, switched on the machine at 'Record' and let it run for a minute.

On playback he found that he had a more than satisfactory recording of Cameron trying and failing to telephone his wife in London. The second stethoscope would act as a monitor. Such improvisations delighted him and he was sorry that they had been superseded by every imaginable kind of electronic gadgetry. Perhaps this was why he so much enjoyed a good detective story: more venturesome than the real thing.

The stage was therefore set. At eight-thirty, knowing that Tom Wood was sitting by Lathan's telephone waiting for Ben-Amir to call, and that there was no danger of meeting him and being recognized by him, Markham emerged from his room. He went to Ben-Amir's suite, ostensibly to see if he was comfortable and had everything he needed, but in fact to relieve Paul Benedict who then went down to the lobby and picked up one of the house-phones. Markham had chosen a house-phone in preference to an outside pay-phone, although the latter would have sounded more authentic, because it was just possible that incoming calls for Lathan might already be recorded: in spite of the Arab management's well-known defence of their clients' privacy.

Benedict, who had lived in the country for some years and could imitate Israeli accents of many kinds, asked to speak to Mr Lathan. The ensuing conversation was short. Yes, the message had been passed on to him from Abba Hayil. No, he couldn't come to Jerusalem at once because he had not yet concluded his business at Ashdod. But yes, he could certainly be at the Seven Gates by ... say, ten o'clock next morning.

3

As far as David Cameron and Tom Wood were concerned, the meeting was simply the next step in an absorbing and promising investigation. For Steve Lathan it was more than this; it was a step into the past, and he was by no means sure about the wisdom of taking steps into the past; in his experience, curiosity had killed more than one cat. For five years he had been wanting to meet Rafael Ben-Amir, yet for five years he had done nothing to bring about such a meeting. Fear, or inbuilt caution? He didn't know. Even now he didn't know, when he stood poised at the very tip of the high-diving board. Perhaps it had been erected at the shallow end of the pool; the water was murky, the bottom invisible.

His wife, for whom the meeting was to prove momentous, recognized his mood of mixed excitement and reluctance. The night before, she had again woken suddenly in the instant before he cried out, and had held him tightly like a child until he emerged from the nighmare, face wet with tears. It would have seemed to her odd if he had *not* dreamed on this particular night, and she watched him go to the meeting with a chill sense of dread; but then dread had lurked behind so much of her marriage, and had intensified so alarmingly during the past five days of it, that she was no longer sure of its real meaning.

Rafael Ben-Amir 'arrived at the hotel from Ashdod' at five minutes past ten: which is to say that he descended from the seventh floor to the fourth, and walked along the corridor. He passed a door—Please Do Not Disturb—behind which Tennison sat on the floor, waiting. One stethoscope was in his ears and he was holding it against the wall just above the second which was taped into position on its pencil-mark. He heard Ben-Amir enter the suite; pressed the 'Record' switch.

Neither the American nor the Israeli had changed very much in the five years since they had last met; they greeted each other cordially but with reserve. Wood and Cameron were introduced and the purpose of their visit to Israel explained. Floor-service produced coffee; to the waiter they must have looked like any other group of businessmen settling down to discuss the . . . the exporting of grapefruit, perhaps. When he had gone Ben Amir said, 'The *truth* about old Isaac's death, eh? Dangerous—you know that.'

Wood said, 'We don't have to mention your name if you . . .'

'You *must* mention my name. It's the only reason I'm here.'

Lathan was surprised by this. 'I don't understand.'

'I've always been in danger—how great I'm not sure. Because I might talk as I'm doing now.' He gestured towards the two Englishmen. 'How much do they know?'

'The physical set-up at the hotel, the security procedures, the little I actually saw of his death. Everything I know myself.'

'Were you instructed by your . . . by The Company not to discuss this?'

'Yes, in a general kind of way. But after six months, when I came out of hospital . . . it all seemed to be over, almost forgotten. There were other jobs.'

'What made you change your mind now? So much later?'

'I'm not sure. First of all, these guys came along, asking questions. And I guess I've always been curious about what really happened.'

The black eyebrows were raised, the black moustache smoothed this way and that. Lathan realized that if he wanted the man's confidence this wasn't enough. Haltingly he added, 'Also . . . after I was wounded I had . . . problems. Mental problems. I still do. I think I owe it to myself, my wife even more, to . . . try and sort them out. I think if I could know the truth . . .' He shrugged.

'I was specifically ordered to say nothing.'

'What made *you* change your mind?'

'My own safety. Once I've said what I know and it's been made public—' a glance at Cameron and Wood—'then I think I'm safe.' A flash of white teeth in the sun-darkened face. 'It's a gamble, everything's a gamble—and the alternative has gone on long enough.'

Lathan was gazing at him, bewilderment in the honest eyes. 'Did you quit or did they push you out?'

'A little of each. After Erter they didn't really want me—and in a way I didn't want them. I'd been trained in irrigation, in the old days I sometimes used it as a cover.' He spread a large hand. 'And you?'

'Roughly the same. I had to choose between getting married and staying on.'

'They were—what's your phrase?—mutually exclusive?'

'In this case, yes. I wonder what happened to my old boss, Gordon McKenna?'

'Promoted.'

Their eyes met for a moment. Lathan frowned. 'Are you sure?'

'Yes. He's now head of the Tokyo station.' He turned to

the two silent journalists; the abrupt change of subject was very noticeable: 'What do you want to ask me? I must tell you I know very little.'

Cameron looked up from his notes and said, 'Mr Ben-Amir, every morning in Rome you used to bring Isaac Erter to the hotel—correct?'

'Yes.'

'You took him as far as these glass doors which led to the passage, and there you handed him over to the Americans. To Mr Lathan, in fact.'

'Yes.'

'What was wrong with that procedure?'

Ben-Amir sat forward. 'Wrong? I don't follow you.'

'Something must have been wrong or you wouldn't have asked for the drill to be changed.'

The big man looked at Lathan, frowning. 'What does he mean? What change is he talking about?'

Wood said, 'Perhaps it wasn't you who asked for it.'

'There was no change.'

Steve Lathan stood up abruptly. 'Gordon McKenna sent for me. It was the evening before. He said I wouldn't be needed in the morning, he said Israeli Intelligence wasn't satisfied with our procedure and wanted to take Erter all the way to the conference table—and since he was your man there was nothing he could do about it.'

Ben-Amir was staring. He tried to speak but apparently found he had no voice. Markham had said, 'Put it another way—you don't know what you know.'

'McKenna told you this?'

'Sure. That's why I wasn't there.'

'You . . . You weren't there because you were sick—you had eaten bad mussels in Trastevere.'

There was a dead silence, broken only by the distant sounds of Jerusalem: a bellowing and squeaking of many motor-horns, a jangle of bells from one of the towers, both reminding the faithful of their mortality. In this silence the shadowy figures of doubt, deceit, treachery began to materialize in the corners of the room, muttering together.

Lathan said, 'Jesus Christ! Who told you that?'

'McKenna. He called me at my office. He said you were ill, I know he mentioned Trastevere and bad mussels. He told me that in your absence I was to hand Erter over to . . . What was his name—your man with red hair?'

'Hamilton.'

'Yes, Hamilton.'

'But he wasn't on duty. I . . . I'd dismissed them all for the day.'

'None of the others were there, but *he* was—waiting by the door where you always stood. He unlocked it and Erter went through. Of course I'd told the old man not to expect you—he liked you, liked seeing you each morning.'

Again silence. Lathan began to move about the room, but jerkily as if unsure of his balance. The unseen shadows were everywhere now; he made a strange movement as if to dispel them, and wheeled around to face the three other men. The brilliant eyes were glittering in a face which had suddenly grown ten years older. 'Jesus God! Do you know what you're saying?'

'It's the truth, my friend. Hamilton was in your place. He took charge of Isaac Erter and locked the doors as you always did.'

'But,' said Cameron, 'who knows this? Did you tell the Inquiry?'

'Of course. When I'd handed Erter over I turned away and left the lobby with my six men, as I did every morning. There were double doors this thick, and you know how noisy the traffic is in Rome . . . We didn't even hear the shooting. Then somebody shouted to us and we ran back. The glass door was smashed and there were people running in the corridor. I saw you—' a glance at Lathan—'I couldn't think why you were there—lying on the floor with Erter on top of you, both covered in blood. I thought you were both dead.'

Incredulously Wood said, 'And the Inquiry knew all this?'
'Every word. More.'
'Then he . . . The CIA killed him.'
'They fired the guns, yes, but our governments killed him. America and Israel, both were guilty.'
'Why?' Lathan was gripping the back of an armchair as if it alone was keeping him on his feet.
'You know that as well as I do. The Americans thought the old man was a Communist—and he hated Communism as much as he hated war. They thought that if he won his case the way would be wide open for Moscow. My own government was . . . just terrified of him. Most of them were pro-war—most of them are still in the Knesset. But if Erter had won they'd have been out, no more power.'
'And we . . .' Lathan gave a gasp, something between laughter and tears. 'You and I, we were the . . . the clowns, the fall-guys.'
'Yes, I see that now. Why else were we pushed out of our respective services? Why else is your Mr McKenna head of a station?'
Wood said, 'But the Official Inquiry, what did they make of all this?
'They made chicken with dumplings. It was so easy—they accepted my evidence and did nothing about it, they just let people think I'd been working with his killers all the time. It didn't matter. All that mattered was that Isaac Erter was dead and couldn't make any more trouble.' He spread both large hands. 'In the interests of security no public statement will be made.'
The crash made them all turn abruptly. Steve Lathan, still clutching the dead body of Isaac Erter, still fighting with a jungle of indoor plants which threatened to devour him, had lost his grip of the chair, fallen forward over the coffee table, now lay face downwards in a mess of broken cups.

4

When Ben-Amir got back to his own suite he found Anthony Markham waiting for him, Benedict still in attendance. Markham had already spoke to Tennison and made sure that the necessary revelations had been made. The two men looked at each other with wholly different kinds of interest. Ben-Amir said, 'I see what you were talking about—why they didn't want us to meet.'

'Simple, wasn't it? Their plans usually suffer from being too complicated.'

'The whole thing could easily have been exposed there and then.'

'With Lathan in hospital and you having taken the vow of silence—and the Official Inquiry venal anyway?' He shook his head.

'It's been exposed now.'

Markham shrugged. Ben-Amir did not bother to ask him why he had gone to so much trouble to ensure that exposition; he knew he would get no answer. He merely said, 'I'm tired of this room.'

'You can go any time you like. They know.'

The Israeli stared at him, warily.

'Benedict here has useful friends. One of them's a cut-out, yours not the Americans'. He passes information, at a price. They know you've had this meeting, but they think it was last night. So . . . you're defused.'

'Thank you.'

'Not at all—my part of the bargain. When those two boys come up with their story you'll be doubly secure, and our friends will have plenty of other things to worry about. How's Lathan?'

'Better. Sitting up and talking.'

Steve Lathan was indeed talking; he lay back on a sofa,

answering all questions with gusto and giving a great deal of information on subjects about which Cameron and Wood were too ignorant to question him. A tape-recorder stood on the table between them. He had found out who it was who had hit him, and was now, as he had said he would, hitting them right back. It went on for an hour. Then he excused himself, saying he'd had enough but was available any time they wanted more enlightenment.

When he stood up, he had to grip the arm of the sofa for support, but once he was on his feet he felt better, perfectly in control once more; no, he didn't want either of them to go with him, it was bad enough scaring them half to death by passing out like a delicate young lady at the sight of blood.

As soon as he'd left the room the two journalists turned to each other with shining eyes. Wood said, 'My God, what a story!'

'Can we bash it out for this Sunday? Or is that too quick? We don't want to wreck it.'

'Deadline tomorrow? No problem. Lick it into shape today, polish it tonight, get Lathan's go-ahead first thing in the morning, and we're off. We'd better call Williams right now—he can tell Attila to hold space.'

Their excitement was contagious, even over the telephone on a questionable line. Their Editor, not given to showing what he felt, grew noticeably enthusiastic as they talked: sometimes both at once, Cameron on the bedroom extension. There was only one real fear, and Wood voiced it: 'Are we in trouble with Official Secrets?'

'You checked that with Clive Marshall.'

'But we never thought it would be this big—I don't think he did either.'

'I'm printing it.' Alistair Williams was staring out of his window at cold grey London, hooded eyes half-closed, anticipating complications and circumventing them in advance. 'Marshall asked around Whitehall, you told me so.'

'Yes. "No objection to Erter, not a dicky-bird," that's what he said.'

'So whoever knows the truth isn't worried. And somebody knows all right—the Americans don't tell our government much, they've got too much sense, but they must have told them the result of that half-baked inquiry. So Whitehall knows and Whitehall gave you the green light.'

'And Washington?'

'I'm not Washington's nanny, neither are you. Stop talking, for God's sake, and start writing. If it's longer than usual don't worry—and I'll give it a box, front page centre.' It was obvious that in spite of himself, in spite of his well-known self-control, he was as excited as they themselves were.

They put the Do Not Disturb sign on the door, dragged in an extra table from one of the bedrooms and settled down to work, Cameron laying out the background and the lead-in to the conference, Wood charting their inquiry step by step: the name Lathan—the Paris address—the first meeting with Mrs Lathan—Lathan himself—the mention of Ben-Amir—Israel . . . It was all good stuff, provocative from the word go. The kind of thing, Cameron allowed himself to think in a momentary pause, that won Awards.

As soon as she saw her husband Holly Lathan guessed what had happened; she knew that drained look, and the blurring around the eyes. She said, 'You would do it, you would come here.'

'I'm glad I did.'

'Lie down, Steve, you look awful.'

'I've *been* lying down. I want to get out of this place. Come on, let's go.'

She didn't ask him what the meeting had brought forth, knowing that he would tell her in his own time; or possibly not tell her, she was used to that. She had watched him go to it with a sense of dread and wasn't in the least surprised to learn that it had knocked him out.

In the crowded, noisy alleyways of the Old City he bought her a straw hat and an outlandish silver necklace, or was it a belt? When he put the hat on her head he kissed her; then said, 'My own people did it, Holly. I was trying to save him from my own people—it was them who just about killed me.' And, searching her face for surprise which wasn't there. 'Yes, I guess you're right, I asked for it.'

Then he took her to the Dome of the Rock, shimmering blue and gold, a dazzling intricacy of design. They sat in shade at the edge of the great stone plateau, watching the faithful wash their feet before entering the mosque. It was all so old and well-worn, so timeless under the timeless desert sun, that nothing else seemed very important. She guessed that he had known this, and had brought her to the place for that very reason.

'You see, they realized how much I liked the old man, how close to him I felt. So I was dismissed. If I'd had any sense I'd have suspected something and stayed away. Or would I? Anyway I didn't have any sense and I didn't suspect anything—I was the lone ranger, and I was right there. Jesus, what a shock that must have given them! The lone ranger galloping in from left field, blazing away with his six-shooter.' He attempted a laugh but it emerged as a gasp of pain. She knew that there was more to come, and it came; suddenly he turned to her, half-hiding his face behind her head, and cried out in a terrible strangled voice. 'Oh God, the bastards! The stupid, corrupt . . . ! Oh, fuck them, *fuck* them!'

She put an arm around him and he rested his forehead on her shoulder, childlike. 'I *believed* in it, Holly.'

'Yes, I know.'

'I thought I was doing something important. For America, for the world, I guess. Sure, I'd heard the stories—the mistakes, poking our noses in the wrong places, financing the wrong people, arming the wrong sides, but . . . I believed in it.' And, with ferocity, 'Not any more!'

He looked up at her sharply because she seemed to have caught her breath. 'What's the matter?'

'Nothing.'

Nothing? She had just realized that possibly, possibly, this death of his belief might contain her own salvation. She tested the incredible idea: 'But Steve, you must have known what it was really like, you must have seen the other side of the coin dozens of times—the ... the arrogance, the double-dealing ...'

'Yes, I saw it. But I ... Okay, I didn't *want* to believe it.' He shook his head savagely. 'I even thought we wanted peace, and Isaac Erter *was* peace, wasn't he? Oh Christ, what a boy scout, what a schmuck, what a prick!'

And, she thought, what a conversation to be having in this particular place: the second most holy place in the Arab world, where Mahommed began his ascent into heaven: the place where Abraham offered up his son in sacrifice! Also the place where idiotic Holly Lathan realized that Providence was perhaps, at last, going to allow her the chance of escape. She tested it again: 'You didn't have any idea it was them?'

'How could I? They fixed me, they used one of my own men, Hamilton, to let him in. Ben-Amir had been told I was ill—he recognized Hamilton and delivered the old man accordingly. Then I guess Hamilton disappeared pretty darn quick, the bastard, and the hit-men took over. Of *course* I didn't recognize them, they'd been flown in from God knows where to do the job.' He stood up abruptly. 'Forget it! That's what I'm going to do—forget I ever had anything to do with the whole goddam shitty outfit.'

He took her hand, and together they walked slowly away from the Rock. He led her through twisting alleys where the old men played backgammon and smoked their nargilehs, through an ever-changing miasma of Middle Eastern smells both fair and foul—spicy food, drains, jasmine, donkey; through cool shadow and pools of scorching sunlight, until they came to the sacred pit in which Jewish faith, anguish, joy, find their apotheosis.

The Western Wall, all that is left to them of the temple of Solomon, was so stark and uncompromisingly bleak, in contrast to the splendours of the Dome and the mosque directly above, that it seemed to be the stone embodiment of a whole people. How could she fail to hear Judith Kollek's voice: 'My country has many faults, oh God, many, many faults, but there is a terrible truth in it.' The wounding stones and the donkey's dung, the foreheads and lips pressed against this indestructible wall of faith. Surely it was here, if anywhere, that she could speak and, with luck, be forgiven. She said, 'Steve, I've got something to tell you—something I should have told you years ago. As bad as . . . what you found out this morning.'

Then she told him: everything, starting at the beginning with her fear of his sexuality, the meeting with Judith Kollek, the spying on him and reporting on him, the falling in love, the terror of losing him, and the absurd, almost criminal lies she had told in order, as she thought, to absolve herself; and then the guilt because he had been forced to give up his job, the pursuing guilt which had led, ineluctably it seemed, to the unknown voice on the telephone, to the blackmail, to Ben-Amir's address, to Israel, to his meeting with Ben-Amir and to his discovery of a bitter truth which, in its turn, had enabled her to admit this truth, more foolish but quite as bitter.

When she had finished there was silence, broken only by the prayers and cries from the Wall. There was no shade. The sun of midday bludgeoned them. She did not dare look at his face, she could only hope. Hope had always existed in this potent place.

Then she felt his fingers under her chin, turning her face towards him. As always, the piercing honesty of the blue eyes surprised her, even shocked her; she would have liked to look away from them but knew that on this of all occasions she must not do so. He said, in a strained and wondering voice, 'My God, what a pair!'

She nodded.

He said, 'It's impossible that anyone could love another person as much as I love you right now.'

Then she knew that she could, indeed must, look away; and did so, closing her eyes, feeling the hot stones heave and buckle beneath her; it seemed that all violent emotions induced vertigo, even this overpowering sense of release. Darkness came and went, leaving her disorientated. She opened her eyes on the blazing glare and felt the sun reaching through to her bones which a moment before had seemed dead and buried.

He said, 'Come on, let's go kiss that wall.'

'But we can't, we're not . . .'

'Know what the Talmud says? It says, "Never has the Divine Presence left the Western Wall." If the Divine Presence is too picky to want a couple of goys . . . Holly, come *on*!'

So they went forward and kissed the Wall, and nobody gave them so much as a glance. Then they went back to the hotel and made love. Neither of them, in their happiness, for one moment considered the danger towards which these twin revelations were already leading.

Later, lying flat on his back and staring at the ceiling, Steve Lathan said, 'If I hadn't been KO'ed by Ben-Amir you wouldn't have been able to tell me, would you?'

'Not now. One day, I suppose.'

He turned his head and looked at her, half-smiling. 'Took us quite a while to get here, didn't it? Talk about Fate moving in a mysterious way!' Then the smile faded, abruptly replaced by consternation: 'Oh God, what about them?'

'Who?'

'Those two poor guys, sitting in there, banging away at their typewriters, thinking they've got the best damn story ever. You'd better tell them right away—can you face it?'

She raised herself and leaned on his chest, searching the loved face with what seemed to her to be new, unshuttered eyes. 'I can face anything, can't I? I'm the world's luckiest stupid bitch.'

Tom Wood and David Cameron were not pleased to be dragged from their precious, their golden, story which was practically writing itself as if driven by some mysterious impulse; but they tried not to show their impatience because, after all, without this man the story might never have been revealed to them. What he and his wife had to say soon put things in a different, not to say alarming, perspective.

'Wait a minute!' said Cameron, owl-eyed behind the strong lenses, curly hair on end. 'You mean . . . You mean this . . . man on the telephone knew all about us, all about all of us?'

Holly Lathan could hardly believe that it was now possible to speak openly of matters which, only an hour before, had been locked into her terrifying Pandora's box. She told them exactly how much the man on the telephone had known: how, after their first meeting at which she had tried so hard to deflect their curiosity, he had blackmailed her into encouraging it.

'Then . . .' Wood choked on his own surprise; tried again: 'Then he . . . he practically *arranged* that dinner.'

'Yes. And he was watching us. He even knew the name of the restaurant, La Cornemuse.'

'Good God! What was he—CIA?'

'No. It sounds crazy but he was sort of protecting us from them. He even warned me that one of their men was following us.'

Lathan said, 'Whatever he was, he was no dummy. He knew that if Holly went to the Israeli Embassy, all that stuff, this guy would tail her there and realize we were trying to contact Ben-Amir.' A gesture. 'Why not? Look what he told us when we *did* contact him!'

Cameron nodded, running both hands through his already wild hair. 'All that business about his being safe once he'd said it—I thought he was dramatizing himself.'

'Hell, no! They'd have killed him all right, if they'd got to him before we did.' A grimace. 'Or maybe arranged for *us* to have a little accident.'

This thought brought with it a moment's silence; then Wood said to Holly, 'Does this mean you never went to the Embassy at all?'

'He told me not to, or we'd all be in danger—he told me to pretend I'd been.'

'But Ben-Amir's address?'

'*He* gave it to me.'

'God, he did know everything.' And, with a glance at Cameron, 'Bet you he had us bugged.'

'Supposing we're bugged here—we ought to find out.'

'Save yourselves the trouble,' said Lathan. 'A, you'll never find it, and B, it's too late—we've talked to Ben-Amir and somebody probably knows every word we said. So what? We have nothing to hide, not any more.' He shook his head disbelievingly. 'Boy! I've known a few set-ups in my time, but this one tops the bill.'

Wood put his head in his hands. Cameron jumped to his feet and began to prowl about the room. 'Where does it start, Tom? How far back does it go?'

Wood groaned.

'I mean that guy in my garage, all that guff about us not being able to get into Israel—and when we arrived at Lod we weren't even on their list.'

'Oh, come on, David, don't get manic. Why would anybody do a thing like that?'

'What effect did it have on us?'

'That's got nothing . . .'

'It's got everything to do with it. Someone's a first-rate psychologist.'

Wood sagged. 'My briefcase too.'

'Of course. What effect did it have, Tom?' He might have dropped the hectoring manner had he been able to guess its outcome.

'Made us more determined than ever.'

'Right.' His pacing came to a sudden halt; he stood transfixed. 'The whole idea, the whole bloody idea! Who *was* the man you met at the Garrick?'

This brought Wood to his feet also. 'No, no, impossible!' But he knew, with sickening certainty, that there was nothing impossible about it.

5

Boyd Braunsweg, Anthony Markham's Nero-when-young, was sitting alone in an office in the Justice Department, tapping his teeth with a golden pencil. He was alone because he believed in keeping people waiting; the more important the person, up to a well-defined point, the longer the hiatus. Jack Monreale, at this moment no doubt enraged at having to kick his heels in an outer office, was very important.

There were four departments, or Directorates as they were properly called, within the CIA: Intelligence, Science and Technology, Management and Services, and Operations, sometimes known as Clandestine Services. The last, comprising as it did the secret agents and all their dubious deeds, was the most prestigious, and Monreale's position within it equally so.

Boyd Braunsweg decided that the waiting had gone on long enough; he wanted the man to know his place, but could not afford to antagonize him. He told the secretary to ask Mr Monreale if he would now be so good as to come in.

Jack Monreale was in his forties, skinny, crew-cut, severe. Like most people in Washington, the President unfortunately excepted, he disliked Boyd Braunsweg but knew that it was necessary, very necessary at the moment, to do business with him.

'Sorry to keep you, Jack. Busy day.'

Monreale, who had about him something of the Italian grand signore which his name implied, didn't bother to answer, sat down without being asked, crossed thin legs neatly.

'Problems, Jack?'

'There's a lot of stuff coming in now, it's piling up.'

'Good! Shows my man's earning his money.'

'Maybe good for you, not for me.'

'How come?'

'Boyd—' extreme patience— 'I'm supposed to pass it all upwards.'

'Unless my memory's flipped we came to a little agreement about that. Anyway, everyone in Washington knows you only report what suits you.'

Operations was an independent-minded Directorate, too independent in the opinion of many, and long overdue for renovation. Its activities were supposedly monitored by various watch-dogs and committees, but the department was not subtitled Clandestine Services for nothing; it had ways of keeping secret those matters which it was unwilling to share.

'What kind of stuff?'

Monreale opened a grey folder. 'This guy in London who gave Lathan's address to the two journalists, he's been transferred.'

'That must have been *days* ago, Jack. You think I'm retarded or something?'

Monreale resisted the urge to tell Boyd Braunsweg exactly what he thought he was. There were more satisfying ways of drawing blood. 'Paris reports that the two guys met Lathan. Seems they persuaded him to go to Israel with them.' He did not mention the fact that the Paris station had known nothing of this arrangement until after the event;

the legend of infallibility must at all costs be maintained. Braunsweg said, 'Better and better.'

'Report from Jerusalem. Yesterday, Ben-Amir, that's the Israeli Intelligence man, disappeared.'

'Jesus! Not killed?'

Monreale smiled. There! It was so easy to cut them down to size; their own fears wielded the knife. He let Braunsweg bleed for a while, adding, 'The story is he had too much sense to want to meet Lathan.' He knew that such an eventuality would put paid to Mr Braunsweg's entire operation, and Mr Braunsweg's face certified the fact. Time to bandage the wound. 'It seems possible that your maverick had something to do with it—may have got there first and snuck him out while no one was looking. If so, he's a smart cookie.'

'He's a smart cookie all right, the son-of-a-bitch!' Braunsweg leaned back in his chair and began playing with the gold pencil. All Washington knew that it had come to him, with matching pen, direct from the Presidential Christmas tree. 'That all you've got to say, Jack?' Sneering contempt now that he had emerged from his crisis.

'I just think you ought to appreciate how dangerous this is—a whole operation going on right under the noses of three tough stations, London, Paris, Jerusalem. If one of them decides to report over my head . . .'

'Quit kidding, Jack. Nobody ever reported over your head, you'd have 'em rubbed out before they could say Star-spangled Banner.'

Monreale laughed. It was an overstated compliment, but as true as made no matter.

Braunsweg didn't like smart-ass laughter. He added softly, 'All this is bullshit, I'll tell you the real reason you're here—you want me to appreciate what a good loyal boy you are, so I won't forget you when it's time to hand out the goodies.'

Rage was not an emotion which Jack Monreale ever

allowed himself to show. As softly, he replied, 'Boyd, somebody already *has* reported over my head.'

Braunsweg dropped the gold pencil. He retrieved it quickly, but the harm was done, the admission made. 'Jesus Christ, what? What does he know?' No need to specify the 'He': not God, but the Director of Central Intelligence.

Only two men in the whole gigantic structure of the CIA were political, the two top men: 'he'—the Director—and his Deputy. As such, they were considered by the active élite, the Monreales, to be complete outsiders, at best despised, at worst ignored.

'He,' said Monreale, 'doesn't *know* anything—but somebody's told him that Lathan's loose in Israel and looking for his Israeli opposite number.'

'Then?'

'He shouted for the Isaac Erter file, just to refresh his memory, and he nearly had a fit.'

'Then?'

'Then he sent for me, naturally. I said I knew all about Lathan being in Israel. And I said I also knew that this guy Ben-Amir had disappeared because he didn't want to have anything to do with him.'

'Smart, Jack, smart as hell.'

'But—' the CIA man tapped his grey folder—'I know more than that, don't I? Not only has Lathan found Ben-Amir but they've talked. The cat, Boyd, is out of the goddam bag.'

'You don't have to tell him that.'

'I can only hold back so long on stuff as strong as this, and it's not forever.'

'Meaning?'

'Meaning, Mr Braunsweg, that your man in Jerusalem had better get his ass in gear, his days are numbered.'

6

As soon as Tom Wood and David Cameron were alone in their own suite, both simmering with the information the Lathans had given them, Cameron became the university lecturer which his father had once hoped he would be; he gave a dissertation, clear-sighted, succinct, above all rational, on the subject of 'Responsibility and The Media', and ended by saying, 'We've got no option, Tom. It's our job to finish this story and make it as good as we can—and that means very good.'

No reply.

'In effect we have to ignore this . . . this whole new facet of it.'

'*Ignore* it!'

'Okay. Put it on one side and come back to it later.'

Wood nodded, staring at the sheet of paper in his typewriter: the description of Steve Lathan, a good description. 'But who's behind it, David?'

'Obviously—somebody who wants the truth published as much as we want to publish it.'

'But why?'

Cameron knew this obdurate tone of old. With growing uneasiness he recalled that argument in their Paris hotel: 'You don't care, do you? You honestly don't care if Lathan *is* ill. If we barge in on him and he has a nervous breakdown or something, that doesn't matter, the only thing that matters is the bloody story!' A trifle desperately, he said, 'Who? Why? Isaac Erter was a . . . a kind of prophet, wasn't he? Thousands of people believed in him—why *shouldn't* one of them, or a group of them, want the truth made public?'

Wood was obviously trying to convince himself that this was a possible solution; as obviously, he couldn't.

Cameron said, 'I tell you what. We'll research the whole

angle when we've finished. It might easily make a damn good sequel.'

Another nod.

'Tom, we're professionals and we've got a deadline. First thing tomorrow morning we're taking this thing to London. They're waiting for it, space laid out, front-page box, the works—and it's the best bloody story we ever had. Now, come on, *let's get on with it!*'

'You're right, of course.'

Cameron raised his eyes to heaven in relief; then turned and sat down at his own typewriter. 'Where have you got to?'

'Lathan in Paris. Description, attitude to his job, laid over the set-up at the hotel in Rome.'

'Read well?'

'Yes, it does. I'll give it to you in about ten minutes.' It sounded like the old routine. Cameron's heart was beginning to beat more slowly; the panic was receding. He glanced over his shoulder. Wood was also sitting now, reading his notes. After a moment he said, 'David? You mean we don't mention any of this stuff with Holly, the voice on the phone, the . . .'

'God, no, it throws the whole shape—we've got a terrific shape.'

'Right.'

'Sequel, remember?'

'Right.' He began to type. The old pattern reasserted itself; they worked in silence, both typewriters rattling. The crisis, if it had been a crisis, was over.

In the next room Tennison, stethoscope to his ears, was deep in thought. After a while he reached for the telephone which sat on the floor at his feet and dialled 414. Markham answered at once: 'Roberts.'

Tennison said, 'Mrs Lathan's come unstuck. She's told them all about me in Paris.'

'Ah!' This was an eventuality which Markham had foreseen. There were few eventualities which he had *not* foreseen, with the possible exception of that hidden one which continued to evade him, slinking about in the darkness at the edges of his mind.

He listened to Tennison intently, grabbing at the salient points like a pike grabbing at grayling: 'We're professionals and we've got a deadline . . . First thing tomorrow we're taking this thing to London . . . Now, come on, let's get on with it!' He controlled the heady sensation of triumph, knowing that it was premature; everything was premature until the finishing-post had been reached, and passed. But the facts remained: the story would break this Sunday: on Monday it would hit the headlines of the world.

'Are they working now?'

'Hard at it.'

'Keep me informed.'

After perhaps half an hour Cameron became aware of a change in the rhythm of his colleague's concentration. The typewriter stopped three times for short periods; then twice for much longer periods. The finished pages, promised a good twenty minutes ago, had not materialized. Now there was prolonged silence from behind him. He turned, hoping to find Wood re-reading what he had written; he wasn't; he was staring out of the window.

Cameron grimaced at the broad back and tried, 'Stuck?'

Wood started, obviously out of deep thought, recollected where he was and what he was doing, and said, 'No, I've finished that section.' He picked up the pages and held them out. Cameron exchanged them for some pages of his own. 'If the info still seems too thick I can spread it about a bit more. Tell me what you think.'

'Sure.'

One of the good things about their relationship, perhaps the best thing about it, was that neither resented the other's criticism; in this area their mutual respect was absolute.

They both read in silence. Soon, a little too soon in

Cameron's opinion, the other man said, 'No, that's great. It grabbed me, even though I knew it all.'

'I haven't finished yours yet.'

'Take your time. I feel a bit . . . woolly, I think I need some fresh air, I'll be back in ten, fifteen minutes.' He went before Cameron could think of anything apposite to say; there was plenty of time, and neither of them minded working all night if need be; they had done it many times before.

It had taken Boyd Braunsweg forty minutes to get through to Jerusalem; the Syrians had blown up something somewhere. He had fired his personal secretary and been rude to her assistant, which meant expensive perfume and even flowers all round: and of course a grovelling apology to get Diane back, he couldn't do without her. By the time he finally reached Markham he was angry and scared, and screaming: 'Do you understand what I'm *saying*? They're *on to* you. The head man's getting information, God knows how. I'm served by morons, *morons* . . . !'

Markham had naturally foreseen that The Company might at some point become aware of what he was doing; he had planned and acted accordingly. All the same, the news, if true, was not reassuring; it settled in the pit of his stomach like uncooked dough.

'For Christ's sake,' shouted the voice from Washington, 'what have you got to be so fucking *calm* about?'

'You pay me to keep calm, Mr Braunsweg. If I behaved the way you're behaving now I'd have been dead years ago.'

'Boy, if you don't get moving and finalize this thing you're going to be dead anyway—jobwise dead, and I'll see to that personally.'

Personal threats did not move Anthony Markham. Moreover, he was locked into a time-capsule, they all were. As patiently as possible he said, 'It'll break on Sunday, it can't break before, you know that as well as I do.'

'Holy cow, we may *all* be dead by then.'

If only the idiot would get off the line and give him time to think. There could be no urgency regarding time, that was self-evident, but there were many other urgencies, and the most important was for thought, as usual: for reviewing all possibilities and taking any precautionary steps which seemed advisable.

'. . . like I said. And get this: I want you to call me every four hours whether there's anything to report or not. I don't think you're capable of running a hamburger-stand, let alone . . .'

Of course the Jerusalem station was aware of the meeting between Lathan and Ben-Amir, because he himself had advised them of it via their bribe-taking cut-out: one of those petty but useful individuals used by all Intelligence agencies who act as go-betweens, knowing nothing except what they're told to say and thus protecting the identity of more important operators.

'. . . but luckily my contact here's a real pro—he's stalling, and so far he's been lucky . . .'

Markham had done this not only to ensure Ben-Amir's safety, part of their deal, but also to explain Lathan's presence in Israel. They also knew of the link between Lathan and the two journalists, and might possibly be considering what steps they ought to take in that direction. But in the great bureaucracy of which they were only a small component they would certainly not take any step until and unless ordered to do so from above. And within twenty-four hours the story would be in London, the presses would be moving.

'. . . if you can do that? Answer me, for God's sake!'

Markham, who had not even heard the question, said, 'It's got to be held your end for another twenty-four hours —tell your real pro that. Whatever happens, he must give nobody here any orders—if he's so good at stalling he can stall that one.'

'Listen, I don't take instructions from any . . .'

'Mr Braunsweg, do you understand? The boys are working on their story now, they're flying it to London tomorrow morning, after that it's in the clear. Nothing else is urgent but that's urgent—no orders from your end for twenty-four hours.'

Tom Wood was walking furiously, and it was too hot even for a gentle stroll, though the sun had long since arched overhead and was now dipping towards the unseen Mediterranean.

He had no idea where he was going, but seemed to have entered the Old City by the Damascus Gate. Presently he found himself struggling up the Via Dolorosa in the company of exhausted or perhaps traumatized pilgrims. To escape from them he turned into an alley, came to an Arab café, and drank turgid coffee outside it. Then he continued to walk.

The sweat was pouring off him, and consequently he was pursued by tormenting flies; also by a group of small boys who followed in his footsteps, wondering at his size and height. Judging from the looks he received from passers-by, he supposed that he must appear demented, but Jerusalem was used to demented tourists, the city had been attracting them for more than two thousand years and yet another one would make no difference.

Finally he came to Mount Zion and climbed it, climbed the citadel which had once been David's, and stood looking out over the Holy City: slave of all he surveyed.

Then he trudged heavily away from ancient history and into the King David Hotel (modern history of a kind) where he drank a couple of magnificent Gin Fizzes: followed by a third, and a fourth, and a fifth. Then, head spiralling, he went back to the Seven Gates, opened the door of the suite, and said, 'It's no good, David, we can't do it—we'd better ring London right now and tell them it's off.'

Cameron appeared wild-eyed in the Lathans' sitting-room. He said, 'Tom's refusing to go through with it, for God's sake come and help me.' They didn't ask questions, which could only mean, he later realized, that they had foreseen the possibility more clearly than he had himself.

Wood was wandering about, looking mutinous. He said, 'I'm sorry, I told him not to bother you—there's nothing you can do.'

Steve Lathan assimilated the mood, the slight blurring of the voice. 'You said it was a terrific story.'

'It *is* a terrific story, but who are we writing it for?' And to his partner: 'If you say that's not important I'll throw you out of the window.'

The Lathans exchanged a glance. She said, 'Tom—the man on the phone, he was on our side, he was protecting us.'

'Nice of him! Why?'

'Does why matter? If he'd been the CIA . . .' His face told her that she had a good point, and she followed it up swiftly. 'He was against the CIA.'

Wood shook his head, looking bemused, which he was (five Gin Fizzes), and stupid, which he wasn't. 'A lot of people are against the CIA, Holly, it doesn't automatically make them lovable. The Kremlin's against the CIA.'

Lathan said, 'At least you know it isn't them.'

'Do I? Okay, I don't think it is, but what do we actually *know*? Nothing. Except that somebody, somebody powerful and clever, wants us to write this story—led us by the nose every inch of the way. Yes—' to Cameron—'you were right. The man in the Garrick, and I bet his name's not Merrion, planted the thing inside me like . . . like a bloody pacemaker.' He sat down on the sofa, lay back and closed his eyes. 'God, I hate myself sometimes but I'm stuck with it!'

Lathan sat opposite him and leaned forward. 'You're too goddam straight, that's your problem. If this is how you want to be you should never have become a reporter.'

'Amen, amen,' from Cameron, heartfelt.

Ignoring his colleague, Wood said, 'Hark who's talking! If you were so goddam straight you should never have become a spook. CIA—*you!*'

Lathan sat back, defeated. His wife was astonished to realize that she actually felt sorry for David Cameron. It seemed that clever and devious men, too used to getting their own way, crumpled utterly in the face of such simple logic. She said, 'Okay, let's say you're right—morally right. What about David, what about your career, don't you owe them something?'

Wood nodded and opened his eyes. 'It's a question of priorities. Stop arguing, you all agree with me, you all *know* I'm right.' He sat upright and looked at each of their faces. 'We've been conned, and we can't publish a word until we know who conned us and why. They may be evil men doing it for an evil purpose. Okay, *reductio ad absurdam*, let's say it *is* the Kremlin . . .' He shook his head. 'We just can't do it—God, it's so *obvious!*'

Silence. Cameron went and looked out of the window. Dusk was falling over the Old City, towers and domes dusted with an intense pink light against a darkening sky. Gazing at this, he said, 'Then I'll write it alone.'

Wood was on his feet in a flash. 'No, you won't! What are you talking about?'

'It's the best story I ever had. I'll sit up all night, I won't use a word of your material, and I'll fly it to London in the morning.'

Wood looked at the Lathans. 'He's lost his marbles.' Then he went right up behind Cameron and said, 'We've got a contract, remember? Everything we do together is *ours*. We can write what we like on our own, but *Follow-Up* belongs to both of us equally, and this is a *Follow-Up* story, and if you print one word of it I'll sue you until you *bleed*.'

Cameron seemed to have shrunk; seemed still to be shrinking as they watched him. But Wood hadn't finished. 'What was it our Sainted Editor called you? A sneaky young amoral opportunist. That's you, Cameron, that's you all right—you'd sell your wife and kids if it made a good story.'

At this, not surprisingly, Cameron wheeled around and hit him, a wild disorganized clout which did little more than take Wood by surprise. Steve Lathan, moving with practised speed, grabbed his raised arm and locked it behind him. Tableau: Cameron moon-pale by the window, Wood bent double with the American astride him, Holly Lathan frozen in mid-gasp. Wood said, 'Sorry. You're hurting.'

Lathan released him. He straightened his clothes. 'Thank you. You're a nice guy. Now I'm going out to get pissed.'

Lathan said, 'You *are* pissed.'

'Think so? Hang around—the best, as the poet said, is yet to be.'

7

Following his conversation with Mr Boyd Braunsweg, hysterical in Washington, Anthony Markham had naturally reviewed every aspect of his predicament. He was quite sure that his initial reaction had been the right one: however much they knew or suspected, the Jerusalem station of the CIA would not move without orders from above; and if he could rely on Braunsweg for nothing else he could rely on him to ensure that no order was given, because his own survival and, what was more, the survival of his precious career depended on it.

Markham also knew that the CIA was extremely chary of interfering with the foreign Press; in the past, such interference had rebounded and hit them full in the face. The situation was still, as it had been ever since he left New York two days before, unbalanced and therefore dangerous; but like a well-designed yacht, holed and listing, it was still leading the race and would win it easily, as long as the weather held.

He had just reached this point of reassurance when there was a tap on the door. Tennison clutching the cassette-recorder. Because the adjoining suite was now empty, the Lathans having removed a shaking Cameron in order to keep him company in his distress, and because Tennison could recognize an emergency when he saw, or as in this case heard one, he had decided to report in person. What he and the recorder had to say shattered Markham's reassurance at a blow. He was so unused to insecurity that for a few seconds he found himself struggling with something very like panic. In fury he grabbed this unthinkable emotion and strangled it.

But on another level, revealed at last, he recognized the uneasiness which had been haunting the puppet-master's mind for the past twenty-four hours. He sat very still as he listened to Tennison's evidence, as if he feared that any sudden movement might scare away the evasive creature which had at last crept out of the shadows, showing itself for what it was: Wood. Of course! Wood's inbuilt and often unwanted moral sense which apparently followed him about like a stray mongrel dog, forever returning however hard he kicked it.

God damn the man! At this of all moments! God damn him to hell and back!

Markham's instinct was to jump to his feet and walk furiously around the room, but he never allowed himself this kind of outlet in front of a subordinate. Instead he listened carefully to the recorder which Tennison had placed in front of him.

'*It's no good, David, we can't do it. We'd better ring London right now and tell them it's off.*'

'*It is a terrific story, but who are we writing it for?*'

'*A lot of people are against the CIA, Holly, it doesn't automatically make them lovable.*'

'Somebody clever and powerful wants us to write this story—led us by the nose every inch of the way.'

'The man at the Garrick planted this thing inside me like a . . . a bloody pace-maker.'

'We've been conned, and we can't publish a word until we know who conned us and why. They may be evil men, doing it for an evil purpose.'

'This is a Follow-Up story, and if you print one word of it I'll sue you until you bleed.'

And back full circle to: '*It's no good, David, we can't do it. We'd better ring London right now and tell them it's off.*'

When the tape subsided into a blank hiss: 'And *did* they ring London?'

'No, not yet.'

Markham turned to the telephone at his elbow and dialled. 'Benedict. Please come here at once.'

The two men were both interested and flattered that they were actually being permitted to meet. Each knew about the compartment principle and how closely Markham adhered to it, therefore each could gauge from such a meeting how high they stood in his trust. But these considerations were quickly brushed aside by the master's mood: neither of them had experienced anything quite like it before, but neither was particularly surprised to find themselves face to face with it now. Paul Benedict had guessed, at Lod Airport, something which Tennison had known for a long time: that Anthony Markham's elegant façade concealed a tough and ruthless mercenary, and here was that very man confronting them.

He explained in a few terse sentences that the two young journalists were refusing to go ahead with the story of Isaac Erter's assassination, and then he explained, even more tersely, just how the two young journalists were going to be *forced* to go ahead with it.

*

In an office in Washington, DC, a squat, powerfully built man of fifty was standing in front of what looked like a complicated family-tree. It was headed 'Organization of the CIA'. The man's eyes wandered over the ramifications, catching such esoteric departments as 'Imagery Analysis Service', 'Foreign Missiles and Space Activities Center', 'Office of Logistics'. Away to the right of the diagram, under the sub-heading 'Directorate of Operations—Clandestine Services', things became as it were para-military: 'Technical Services Division', 'Covert Action Staff', 'Field Stations and Bases'.

At the very apex of the immense pyramid stood a single lonely word: 'Director'. The man grimaced at this, for it denoted himself: Judson Masters, Director of Central Intelligence.

His Deputy, younger, slighter, was standing in the room behind him. Without turning, Judson Masters said, 'I had this darn thing made as soon as I got the job—so I'd know who they all were. That was seven years ago, and I still don't know who they all are.' He turned and looked at his Deputy; gave him his Churchillian glare. He had admired Churchill and imagined that he looked like him. 'This guy, Lathan . . . You with me?'

'Yeah. Sure. Israel.' The Deputy DCI spoke in monosyllables as often as possible; he was under the impression that the habit denoted a quick, clear mind. Other people said he did it because it was impossible for a man to make a fool of himself in single words.

The Director of Central Intelligence said, 'Well, I've been making a couple of calls, learning a couple of things. It's a stick-up.'

His Deputy frowned.

'Or if you prefer, I'm being framed.'

'Because of that old business with Isaac Erter?' He too had boned-up on the files.

'No, not because of him, by means of him. Sit down, Fred,

and listen—you may as well know why you're about to lose your job.'

His Deputy sat down, more in shock than obedience.

'When I gave the go-ahead on Erter's assassination I did it in good faith, one hundred per cent. All the research departments indicated that he was soft, a pink liberal, liable to let the Commies in. The Israelis wanted him out, the Pentagon wanted him out, the President wanted him out. Hell, yes, *I* wanted him out too—if we don't have a strong Israel those Arab bastards will take over everything.'

Fred, Deputy Director of Central Intelligence, said nothing.

'Okay, you disagree, you're younger than I am. Times change, by God they do!' He pulled gently at the bottom of the chart which delineated his empire; it rolled up into the ceiling and was gone.

'So I gave the go-ahead, and Isaac Erter was rubbed out and all his half-assed peace baloney with him. In good faith, Fred, don't forget that when you get around to writing your memoirs.' He lit a cigar and puffed at it twice.

'Now . . . By golly, times certainly change! Now we kind of *like* the Arabs, don't we? They've got all the oil—we're kind of tired of baling Israel out—we're kind of crazy in the head, but don't tell the voters that, they think they're the bee's knees. Suddenly all the research departments do an about-turn, and the Pentagon's only interested in who can blow the world apart first, and the President . . . Lordy, Lordy, the President's changed his little old mind, what's left of it, and guess who they want out now? Eh? Eh, Fred?'

'Hell, Jud, I think you've got this screwed up.'

'I don't think any darn thing, I *know* I've got it right, I was in politics when you were in diapers.' He decided he didn't like the cigar and ground it into an ashtray, savagely. 'They want me out, and somehow or other they're using old Isaac Erter to get me out—I guess you could call that retribution.'

'Using? How?'

'I don't know, because somebody's sitting on the information—but I can smell it a mile off, that's what they're doing.'

'They? Who's they?'

'That little shit-head Braunsweg for a start. He can't wait to get his fat ass in my chair.'

'He couldn't do your job.'

'Nobody can do my job, Fred, because the CIA doesn't want anybody to do it—and what's more, a picked team of super-spooks like Jack Monreale is there to see nobody ever *does* do it.'

Something, perhaps the realization that he might indeed be about to lose his job, now jolted the Deputy DCI into consecutive speech. 'You talk as if you're just going to sit and take it, Jud, you've got to fight back.'

The older man shook his head. 'Let me tell you something, you can hang it over your bed—don't ever pick a fight with the Pentagon, the President, or History, they all fight dirty. As for the job, Shit-head Braunsweg can have it, it'll kill him.'

On the other side of Washington, Shit-head Braunsweg, dishevelled and sweaty, was circling another office like a caged cat or, as Anthony Markham might have thought, like the young Nero having one of his bad turns.

Senator Jefferson Drysdale, perching on the edge of a giant desk, watched him with dispassionate interest. He was wondering whether this really was the right man to replace Judson Masters as Director of Central Intelligence: even if everything worked out, even if the President seemed sure of the choice. He said, 'You'll have to learn to ride the wave, Boyd, or you'll bust a gut—Washington will see to that.'

'Ride the wave! I call the guy and he tells me these dumb Limey journalists are refusing to write the story—Jefferson, do you realize what that *means*?'

'As well as you do.' It could even mean that he, Jefferson Drysdale, might have to put up for several years with the present Director blocking him and denying him information at every turn: the very idea made him feel sick. At least this unpleasant young man pacing about the room wouldn't block him; couldn't *afford* to block him in view of what he would know about the young man's accession to power. A shade less dispassionately, he said, 'Have to sweat it out, Boyd, nothing else you can do.'

An old vulture perched on the edge of a desk: or, more properly, an old vulture sitting on the fence, waiting to see which body was going to fall where, providing his next meal.

8

By the time David Cameron reached his third Scotch on the rocks, colour had returned to his cheeks and some of the old self-confidence to his personality; he had even joined battle with the Lathans on the subject of morality, claiming that certain people, journalists among them, simply couldn't afford the luxury of an ethical conscience as other people understood it. Lathan was arguing that anyone whose job involved information or instruction couldn't afford *not* to have an ethical conscience. His wife said that they were both talking large Scotches-on-the-rocks: half the people in the world didn't even know the meaning of the words 'conscience' or 'ethic' and cared a great deal less.

At this point the telephone rang: a distraught hotel receptionist trying to find Mr Cameron. 'Sure, he's right here.'

Cameron took the receiver, listened, paled all over again, said, 'Oh God!' twice, and then, 'All right, I'll come, I'll come at once.' He banged down the receiver and looked at his hosts. 'It's Tom. He's picked a fight in the bar of the King David, smashed up a lot of stuff. The police are there now.'

He and Lathan grabbed their jackets, for respectability, and ran. In the elevator Lathan said, 'Has this happened before?'

'Only once—in Berlin. Same reason.'

'Conscience?'

'He hates the bloody thing, that's the point.'

'Wouldn't be the guy he is without it.'

'He'd be a hell of a lot easier to work with.'

It was only ten minutes' walk to the King David but they needed to get there quicker than that: straight into a waiting taxi.

Lathan said, 'We shouldn't have let him go out on his own.'

A snort from Cameron. 'Try stopping him some time.'

It seemed to Holly Lathan that they had only just gone when the doorbell rang. Geared to emergency she ran to the door and opened it. The man who stood there said, 'Good evening, Mrs Lathan, I wonder if you recognize me—I should say, my voice?'

She had, immediately. And the shock was so great that she allowed him to walk past her into the room; then, not having had the advantage of her husband's training in such matters, she turned to face him, turned her back on the open door. While Tennison was saying, 'I'm very sorry to intrude on you like this . . .' Paul Benedict came in quickly behind her. He was wearing a monogrammed green apron, as issued to hotel staff, over white shirt and dark trousers; he threw one arm around her, strapping her to his muscular body, and put the other one over her mouth. She struggled frantically but might as well have saved herself the effort. Anthony Markham had followed Benedict. He shut the door.

Tennison freed one of her arms and held it taut. Markham, who had produced a hypodermic syringe and a swab, wiped her arm and inserted the needle with practised skill. Even before she had time to experience the nausea which injections of any kind always aroused in her, the room began to undulate and revolve, growing rapidly darker.

Markham had timed this section of the plan at one and a half minutes, but it had not even taken that long.

What was happening in the street below was, from his point of view, less satisfactory, and it accorded to no plan: the regrettable human factor again. As the taxi, with Lathan and Cameron tense inside it, shot away from traffic-lights, Cameron suddenly choked, staring, and shouted, 'Oh my God! Stop! *Stop!*'

The taxi-driver, who in any case thought he had undertaken a couple of intoxicated and possibly crazed foreigners, pulled across to the kerb amid the usual fanfare of hostile horns and a few choice expletives. But long before he reached it, Lathan had seen the cause of Cameron's convulsion: Tom Wood ambling towards them, looking into shop windows.

At about this moment Benedict, who had returned to the corridor, came back into the room wheeling one of the large plastic-lined baskets in which, every morning, a small army of men dressed as he was now, in shirt, dark trousers and monogrammed hotel apron, removed dirty sheets and towels. He took an armful of linen out of it. Markham and Tennison lifted Holly Lathan's limp body and placed it carefully in the basket: no unnecessary rough behaviour in Markham's organization. Benedict covered it with linen. Tennison had already opened the door.

Steve Lathan, followed by Wood and Cameron, burst into the lobby and ran across it. Several well-heeled tourist matrons clutched purses to their stomachs or jewels to their throats in a communal reflex action of our times, but by and large nobody even noticed the three men. There was an elevator waiting; they plunged into it. The elevators at the Seven Gates were new and swift, but this one seemed weary and unwilling to ascend.

At the fourth floor they shot out of it and ran straight past Tennison who didn't even blink, let alone call out a warning, shocking though their appearance was at this juncture. He had long since been trained to accept that the plan was everything; warnings only deflected the plan, even impeded it for the irretrievable few seconds which separated success from failure. He pursued his own small part, entering the elevator and pressing button B for Basement; then put his finger on Door Close and held it there.

As Lathan, Wood and Cameron turned a corner in the corridor and ran towards the suite they saw (but did not see because it was so usual a sight) one of the hotel's male employees, little more than a kind of male chambermaid, wheeling a dirty-linen basket away from them. Then he too turned a corner and was gone.

It didn't take more than a few seconds and an unanswered shout for them to realize that Holly had disappeared. Wood immediately recollected the man wheeling the basket; he pointed. 'Down there, going away from us.'

As soon as he had turned the corner Benedict started running; he hadn't glanced over his shoulder and was therefore not sure what was going on behind him: hurrying feet, certainly, and agitated men's voices.

Markham was standing by the service elevator, holding open its gate, the kind with a trellis-like folding grille. Benedict pushed the trolley into it. Markham slammed the gate and, hearing running footsteps, turned swiftly and pushed through double swing-doors—Fire Doors, Keep Closed—moving towards the guest elevator.

Wood, followed by Lathan, followed by Cameron, reached the service elevator a few seconds after Benedict had pressed button B for Basement. The elevator, which was heavy and slow, began to descend. Lathan, wishing for perhaps the tenth time in the last five minutes that he had a gun, turned to a neatly-coiled fire-hose on a rack beside the shaft; grabbed the heavy brass nozzle and swung it savagely at the catch of the folding gate; again; again, and the catch snapped. Wood wrenched the gate open.

At this point some elevators would have come to an automatic halt for reasons of safety; unfortunately this one was not so designed; it continued to descend, reaching third-floor level.

Before Cameron or Wood even knew what he was doing, Lathan had pushed past them, had jumped into the shaft. He landed, sprawling, on the roof of the moving elevator some fourteen feet below. Wood and Cameron looked at each other aghast. Cameron shouted, 'Stairs!' They both turned to the emergency staircase, bare echoing concrete, and went leaping down it.

Markham emerged from the guest elevator into the lobby and walked across it very quickly but in a way which suggested no sense of speed whatever. No matron clasped her purse, though several gave him approving looks: so handsome, well-dressed, purposeful! He pushed through the revolving doors, past the doorman who was about to summon a taxi for him, turned to the left and disappeared among artfully arranged vegetation which screened the hotel's service road.

As he swung into it he saw that Tennison was already standing at the back of the Range-Rover; had already started the motor according to plan.

With only one more floor to go, Lathan had not succeeded in kicking a hole in the slatted roof of the service elevator which had been designed, in this climate, for maximum ventilation; but it was disintegrating fast and therefore enabled him to see that the man below had drawn a gun. Feeling incredibly unprotected, area of the genitalia in particular, he continued to destroy the roof, his only consolation being the knowledge that shots fired from below are seldom fatal.

Luckily for both men, Benedict did not have to shoot. The elevator came to an abrupt halt, throwing Lathan off balance and nearly breaking an ankle because his foot was caught in the sizeable hole it had created. He swung himself upright, gripped the edge of this hole and exerted all his strength. A good quarter of the roof gave way. He was already dropping into the elevator before Benedict, impeded by the spring-action of the gate, had dragged the trolley out of it.

By the time Lathan picked himself up off the floor Benedict was a quarter of the way along the bleak basement passage. At this moment someone somewhere summoned the elevator. It groaned into an ascent. Lathan flung himself at the Stop button, reached it, somehow manipulated the gate with one hand and a leg, and fell out into the passage. The elevator recommenced its majestic ascent.

Collecting himself, he saw that this disruption had lost vital time; Benedict was already pushing the basket up a ramp at the end of the passage. Two maids going about their evening duties cringed against the wall, not so much in fear as to get out of the way of this peculiar circumstance. Both were Arab, both were presumably thinking 'Insh' Allah', a good philosophy for such occasions.

As Lathan sprinted past them he heard Wood and Cameron pounding down the echoing emergency staircase. Benedict had now reached the service road. Tennison took hold of the other end of the trolley and they both heaved the whole thing into the rear of the vehicle. Tennison piled in after it; he still hadn't closed the rear door by the time Benedict reached the driver's seat and pushed the lever into bottom gear. The Range-Rover began to move; no gunning of the engine or screeching tyres, Markham didn't encourage that kind of macho, filmic excess.

Lathan gave chase and, in a sudden vein-bursting thrust of speed, even managed to grasp moving metal, get a firm grip of it, heave his body upwards.

Wood and Cameron emerged from the hotel just in time to catch a horrifying glimpse of the figure which stepped out of deep shadow immediately in front of the accelerating vehicle. The headlights, sweeping over it, did not reveal the man's face, only the fact that he was taking steady aim. He fired, the bullet making little more than an angry hiss.

Lathan was hit. His legs were giving out anyway; they now gave out. He adopted the necessary rolling position, let go and rolled, coming to a painful stop against a row of oil drums.

By the time Cameron and Wood reached him, Markham had disappeared and so had the Range-Rover. Somewhere voices, of hotel staff presumably, were raised in question, not particularly urgent because there weren't many of them about at this time of evening—the plan had relied on that—and in any case the whole incident had been so swift.

Lathan was as limp as a rag doll. The two young Englishmen were both quite sure that he was dead. Then Cameron noticed the small metal dart protruding from his shirt just below the left shoulder.

In the back of the moving vehicle, Tennison removed the sheets and, using them as padding, propped Holly Lathan into a more comfortable position. He was keeping her in the basket for her own safety; Benedict was certainly not an Israeli but, as certainly, he drove like one. Soon they were clear of the city, heading for Tel Aviv.

Tom Wood and David Cameron manhandled Lathan back to his suite, fending off a curious kitchen porter and the two maids who had now found their voices. They shared the elevator with a jolly Jewish gentleman from the Bronx who said with genuine regret, 'Why don't *I* get asked to any of the good parties?'

They heaved Lathan on to the sofa and looked at each other. Wood said, 'Police,' and moved towards the telephone.

Cameron said, 'I'm not sure. Tom, hold it!'

'They'll get clean away with her.'

'But if we put the cops on to them they may panic and . . .' He didn't need to complete the sentence.

A slurred voice behind them said, 'No . . . police.' Lathan was coming round. His eyes were barely open and his speech sounded as if somebody had stuffed a pair of socks into his mouth. He tried to sit up and failed. Wood put a beefy arm under him and lifted him into the upright position. After perhaps a minute he managed to say it again, more firmly: 'No police!'

The eyes were a little wider open now, but the pupils were abnormally large and it was doubtful if he could see anything clearly.

'But,' said Wood, 'maybe they could block the roads out of Jerusalem, there aren't that many.'

Lathan shook his head, which wobbled about in all directions. 'Not . . . Not until we've heard their . . . terms, that's the rule.'

'Correct.' Anthony Markham's voice made Cameron and Wood jerk around as if they were controlled by the same spring.

Markham shut the door—they had left it ajar—and showed them the gun which he didn't consider it necessary to point. 'Sorry about this. Three to one, you see.' It wasn't the kind of gun that fired dainty little darts.

Wood was grimacing to himself. Cameron said, 'Friend of yours from the Garrick, I presume.'

Wood nodded.

Markham gave a grim smile. 'Don't blame yourself, I've conned better men than you.'

It would be wrong to say that they had forgotten Lathan, simply that in the shock of Markham's appearance they weren't looking at him. In any case what he now did was so out of character, his character being temporarily absent, that it was inconceivable. He found strength from somewhere, shot straight out of the sofa and literally threw himself at Markham.

Markham let out a grunt of pain, thudding back against the door, and it was possible in those few seconds that if the other two had also been trained by the CIA they might have overpowered the man and got his gun away from him.

But to what end? None. The end was a missing girl.

When the flailing of arms and legs subsided Markham was seen to be holding a faintly struggling Lathan clear of the floor with both arms, the gun now protruding from one of his armpits. Then he released him, and Lathan fell in a heap at his feet.

Markham said, 'Put him back on the sofa. Sit on him or something.' He had timed his entrance to coincide with Lathan's recovery; fifteen minutes it had said on the capsule and fifteen minutes it had been, exactly; the man must have incredible physical stamina to do what he had just done. 'Good thing I'm not trigger-happy!'

Lathan now lay back, panting, spent. 'What about . . . my wife?'

'She's a hundred per cent safe. No harm will come to her, none at all.'

'If?'

'You know all that. If your friends here get moving and write that story.'

'And if they don't?'

'She'll be killed and buried somewhere out in the desert.' There was no mistaking the certainty of this, made more certain by extreme equanimity.

'Other terms?'

'As you were saying, no police. They'd never find her anyway, and if there was any chance of it I'd fly her out of the country. But that's a lot of hassle, we don't need it.'

Cameron burst out, 'What *is* all this anyway? What does Isaac Erter mean to you? Why take it out on us?'

'If you go about asking loaded questions you must expect a few loaded answers.' Markham weighed the gun in his hand; then hitched it loosely into his pocket, easy to reach.

Lathan sat upright, made an effort to stand again but couldn't find the strength. However, his brain was evidently back in working order. 'There is another deal, you know.'

'Really? You're ahead of me.'

'You've gone to a hell of a lot of trouble to . . . to kick The Company in the face, haven't you?'

'There's nothing for you there, they know all about it.'

'You've planned it like a military operation, every darn thing in its place.'

'Nobody's ever accused me of being inefficient.'

'Come to think of it . . . Yes, I bet you set up Rafael Ben-Amir too.'

'He'd never have spoken to you if I hadn't.'

'All to screw the CIA and keep them out of the picture. Boy! that really matters to you, doesn't it?'

'Does it?'

'Yes, like hell. So how's this? If you don't get my wife back in this room, and I mean fast, I'm going to the Jerusalem station and I'm telling my old friends up there every goddam thing I know. I'll spill enough beans about you to feed the whole of Texas on chilli for a year.'

Markham nodded. 'You will, uh?'

'I sure will. I don't know why you want this story published so badly—you don't look like an Isaac Erter fan to me—but *they*'ll know, and my hunch is you'll be in the shit right up to your neck.'

Markham seemed to be considering this: or at least some aspect of it. Encouraged by his silence, Lathan said, 'You return my wife, like now, like pick up that phone and start giving orders, or I go to the CIA at once, no kidding. That's *my* deal.'

After a time Markham nodded again, but curtly. 'When this is all over I'll send you my contact number in New York. If you ever get tired of Lagarde et Rochet come to me —you've got brains and guts and style, and I pay twice your present salary.' He turned towards the door.

Lathan said, 'I mean it.'

Markham looked back at him. 'No you don't, you're still

high on Prolitherin. One: you hate their guts. They killed Isaac Erter and it's just Lathan's luck they didn't kill you —go to them now and they probably will. Two: you don't know a thing, not even as much as they do and that's peanuts. Three: tell them anything you like, you're not getting your pretty wife back until the story's in print.' He looked at the two reporters and added, 'Give him plenty of coffee, no alcohol—and start writing, for God's sake, it's still the biggest break you ever had.' With which he was gone.

There was a long silence. Lathan lay back again and closed his eyes; he felt sick. 'Hit the nail bang on the head, didn't we, Tom? You never should have been a mediaman, I never should have been a spook.'

Wood sighed deeply. 'Bit late to change that now.' He glanced at his partner. 'Jesus, look at this creep! Face as long as a yard of piss, and underneath it he's grinning from ear to ear.'

'That's right, take it out on me!'

'You can stand it—you've won, haven't you?'

'Teach you to be careful where you find your great story ideas.'

'Oh God!'

Lathan said, 'I'm sorry, Tom.'

'What do you mean, *you're* sorry? Who got you into this? I did.'

'I'm sorry because it was a great idea – not writing the story, not being . . . led by the nose, not letting them have their own way.'

Cameron said, 'Who do you think they are anyway— who's he?'

'God knows. I guess we'll find out when you're in print.'

Wood said, 'Will she be all right, do you trust him?'

'Sure, I trust him. He's an operator, an intelligent one— they don't make silly mistakes.'

Wood shrugged and sighed again. 'Well . . . I said it was a question of priorities, and she's our Number One priority now.' He headed for the door. 'Come on, Sweeney Todd, let's get the bloody thing written.'

Cameron grimaced at Lathan and followed him.

9

Tom Wood and David Cameron finished writing their story on the assassination of Isaac Erter in the small hours of the following morning. Steve Lathan read it and suggested a few alterations which Wood retyped while Cameron was packing his suitcase.

Cameron then flew to London. Wood stayed with Lathan to lend him moral support during the endless twenty-four hours of waiting.

The story appeared under the *Follow-Up* heading in Sunday's newspaper and caused a furore even in Britain. An hour later Holly Lathan arrived in a taxi at the Hotel of the Seven Gates. The Range-Rover had taken her to a small house set in the middle of citrus groves, nothing else as far as the eye could see. That was all she knew, except that her bedroom had been equipped with a barred window and she had been treated with exceptional courtesy by her two guardians. The man to whom she had spoken on the telephone in Paris spent most of his time reading, and a younger man, Jewish, bearded, turned out to be a dedicated chess-player. He had improved her game considerably.

On the following morning, Monday, there was hardly a newspaper in the world that didn't carry the story on its front page under banner headlines, in spite of the fact that television had already given it maximum coverage: Isaac Erter, man of peace, had been murdered not by unknown Arab terrorists but by the CIA acting on behalf of the governments of the United States and Israel, for once in complete agreement.

Reaction was immediate and sometimes violent. Supporters of Isaac Erter—many, many more of them than he had ever commanded in his lifetime (but that wouldn't have surprised him)—came swarming out of the hives of their own forgetfulness and surged about the streets of half the world's capital cities.

The current Israeli Government lost a vote of confidence and collapsed in ruins: soon to be rebuilt, no doubt, in exact replica, give or take a few unimportant details.

The President of the United States was attacked from all sides, and had it been election time, which of course it wasn't, he would have collected a mere handful of Jewish votes and none at all from the vast numbers of Americans who were vaguely in favour of peace. Even people who had hated Isaac Erter now loved him; after all, he was dead and could no longer rock the boat. The President, needless to say, cried 'Not guilty,' and pointed his finger at the CIA.

Judson Masters, Director of Central Intelligence, escaped to his office from the baying hounds of the media, unrolled for the last time his huge chart of the organization, and wrote with a red-tipped felt pen, next to the meridianal title 'Director', the words, 'Poor stupid son-of-a-bitch!'

Boyd Braunsweg gave a discreet champagne party to his closest friends and other useful people. Senator Jefferson Drysdale did not attend, he was drinking a Martini with the President. They decided that Braunsweg might as well be given the job; after all, he had managed, at considerable expense, to get rid of that secretive and therefore dangerous autocrat, Judson Masters, and his illegal manner of doing so ensured that he himself could never afford to be secretive, dangerous or autocratic, and would at all times do exactly as he was told.

Anthony Markham read about all these momentous events

while sitting beside the pool of his house in the hills above Santa Barbara, California. His wife, grown tired of interminable and unexplained absences, had long since divorced him on grounds of cruelty and desertion, but she had fortunately remarried. The beautiful woman with whom he now shared the rare moments of his private life was a painter, perfectly content to be left alone with her all-absorbing art while he practised his elsewhere.

She knew that he took grave risks and spent much of his time breaking the law in various countries, but that was the kind of man he was, and that was why she loved him. Also, on a more practical level, her painting would not have kept them both in the most miserable garret, whereas his activities kept them both in luxury, and in the kind of seclusion which has become the greatest luxury of all.

It was typical of a Markham operation that nobody but himself and two men in Washington knew the whole story of what he had accomplished, and how, and why. (The compartment principle again.) When Steve Lathan read in the *International Herald Tribune* that there had been sudden and unexpected changes at the very top of the Central Intelligence Agency he wondered if by chance he had stumbled on the motive; but neither he, nor Messrs Wood and Cameron, who were also interested in the news, could do more than wonder; after all, such political power games mean little to ordinary men even though they are the ones who are used, and sometimes killed, in order to satisfy the vanity or ambition of the people who play those power games.

Tennison, it is true, had a pretty good idea of what had been going on, but then Markham would never have trusted him if he wasn't a sensible man who knew that it was no part of his well-paid job to ask questions or to have ideas. He returned, as he always did between assignments, to his widowed sister who lived in dull respectability at one of Britain's dullest seaside resorts. Here he read the latest detective stories, kept himself in physical trim, and occasionally visited a plump and genial blonde called Patsy whom he had been courting, to use the euphemism, for some years.

Benedict went back to the snug bosom of his family in Whitechapel in the East End of London, where he added one or two new items to his extensive and valuable collection of firearms, and where, perversely, but he was nothing if not perverse, he always wore the kapel which he declined to wear in Israel.

Rafael Ben-Amir stayed with Ruth at Abba Hayil in order to complete the work which needed to be done there. Such people, who are the backbone of that country, do not shirk responsibility because of a little discomfort; and at least he is now able to work in safety.

Steve Lathan returned to Industrial Peace at Lagarde et Rochet, but Holly has given up her job with Golden Promotions because she is expecting a baby. Freedom from guilt is still a constant wonder to her, and she is still grateful to the mysterious circumstances, and the equally mysterious men, who offered her a means of escape.

Indeed, she is grateful for more than that, because her husband no longer seems to be haunted by nightmares and headaches; moreover, it is now a year since last he suffered one of those alarming collapses: in the Hotel of the Seven Gates.

Occasionally, when Industrial Peace becomes too peaceful, he takes a look at Markham's contact number in New York which, true to his word, Markham sent him; but so far he has managed to resist any temptation it may offer, and he doesn't forget that he now has a family to consider.

Tom Wood and David Cameron, having earned acclaim, two awards, and a handsome sum of money from the *Follow-Up* story on Isaac Erter's death, are busy writing a book about their experiences in Paris and Jerusalem. They argue a good deal about the moral attitude it takes upon certain subjects, but it seems certain to be a bestseller.

As for Isaac Erter himself, his ashes are buried in a cemetery near the kibbutz where he spent his idealistic youth. Many people, looking at the world about them, may be forgiven for thinking that Peace, for which he died, was buried there with him.